PRINCE ANAK

THE IMMORTAL

MATTHEW P. SCHMIDT

O&H Books

Prince Anak the Immortal
Copyright © 2013 by Matthew P. Schmidt. All rights reserved.
Second Print Edition: July 2017

Author Blog: smithgift.wordpress.com
Publisher Website: oandhbooks.com

ISBN-10: 0-9960057-2-2
ISBN-13: 978-0-9960057-2-2
Published by O and H Books LLC

Cover and Formatting: Streetlight Graphics

To St. Dismas

PROLOGUE

The Ixotak war carrier fleet, *The Victorious Strokes of Light,* arrived in Earth's solar system, the twenty-first of September of 1963, almost a year after the Cold War became the Final War. Their probes discovered a ruined planet and a nearly-extinct intelligent race.

Millions had perished on October 27, 1962, when the Cuban Missile Crisis ended in nuclear war. Radioactive fallout poisoned millions more. Farm animals and crops died in the nuclear winter, and starvation claimed more lives. Worldwide rioting, looting and anarchy followed as the sick, hungry survivors battled each other for the remaining food.

The Ixotak had entered Earth's solar system in the ever-expanding front against the Foe. The Foe was sure to arrive soon, as well, with its own war carriers and their ravenous, self-replicating machines. With both the destruction of Earth's biosphere and the incoming threat from the Foe, Ixotak Twenty-Five-Admiral Aizokek made the painful judgment that the only way to save mankind was to evacuate Earth.

Their newfound task was nearly impossible. The Ixotak war carriers had no room for the humans. Earth's gravity demanded a massive expenditure of energy for the smallest mass to escape, and the Final War had demolished the humans' early attempts at rocket science. The few survivors were scattered across the entire planet. Furthermore, the kinetic-magnetic language of the Ixotak was incomprehensible to the humans.

The Ixotak attacked these problems with ingenuity. Using infrared scanners they discovered survivors where they could, but there was too much Earth to search. After attempts at direct communication proved futile, the Ixotak sent robots with holographic images to convey their intent. Still, many survivors did not believe or understand them. Hundreds of carbon nanotube space elevators were built to carry those willing off Earth. Massive space arks were constructed from lunar minerals to hold the survivors. Yet the Ixotak knew that even at maximum speed, they could not transport all of Earth's remaining population before the Foe arrived. The arks soon became overcrowded, taxing the limits of the life support systems.

Barely three months later, the Foe arrived. The Ixotak were forced to defend the arks' retreat. Despite their valor, some arks were lost in the desperate battle while Earth was bombarded by the Foe with asteroids. By the time the Ixotak had escaped, the only living humans were aboard the arks, a fraction of the previous human population.

The Ixotak gave the weary human refugees a home on one of their abandoned outposts within the solar system they called "The Third Drop of Poison." Twenty-five deserted, massive city-monoliths protected the survivors from the planet's poisonous, stormy atmosphere. The planet was soon dubbed "Refuge" by the humans, and the city-monoliths, "arcoliths." True interspecies communication was finally established. Then the Ixotak left, keeping only in brief contact with humanity.

Eighty years passed. The Third and Fourth Generations of humans built new nations with new dreams and new technology. The Lauriel Genetic Federation, based in Lauriel's Arcolith, genetically engineered a new species, *Homo Immortalis.* An immortal king ruled the LGF, and at his behest, in an underground facility far from the arcoliths, a young immortal prince worked on a secret project.

CHAPTER ONE

PRINCE ANAK OG ELOI XIA11 was simply delighted. The result of three years of hard labor, thousands of man-hours by Ph.D-level physicists, engineers, nanotech programmers, and skilled technicians, and billions of credits in robotics and nanobots was now complete. He had already made his speech to general applause. All that was left was to give the word.

There were not enough chairs in the control center, even if there had been room for them. Everyone with enough clearance waited inside to watch the fruit of their labors. Anak had his two guards. The air grew hot and stale.

Almost everyone was wearing green uniform jumpsuits from Lauriel's Arcolith. Some wore uniforms from Rororo, Tanihek, and Xem, and there was one in the black cape and cap of Zozil. The colors clashed though everyone there shared the same purpose.

Anak himself wore his usual green fur robes, the same unnatural bright lime-green of his eyes. The robes were exceedingly long as Anak at sixteen was nearly two meters tall. His blond-haired head bore a small, synthetic emerald-studded circlet.

Today's activation was actually the third attempt to bring the facility online. The first had been scuttled by a small leak in one of the coolant pipes. A broken electromagnet in accelerator five ruined the second. But everyone was still hopeful that *this* time it would all work.

Technicians, no less than fifteen of them, worked to full readiness. The fusion reactors were already running as well as several other systems. At last the supervisor said, "We're ready, sir."

"Excellent," Anak said. "Activate!"

The technicians, to cheers, began pressing keys and entering voice commands. Deep beneath them the vast machinery awoke. There was no satistifying rumble, no loud hum, no change in sound at all except for the holding of breaths. But they knew what was happening, Anak most of all.

Particles collided with unimaginable energy. By application of Einstein's famous equation, that energy became matter-antimatter pairs. Special magnets guided the newborn antiprotons into deceleration machines. Paired with positrons from another set of machines, the antiprotons formed the substance known as antihydrogen. More machines placed the antihydrogen into the magnetic fields of the Bowyer Traps, special containment units of perfect vacuum.

Within a split second after the process reached full speed, more antimatter than the entire human race had ever produced elsewhere was created and stored. Within half a second, they had already made over a microgram of antimatter, an amount so tiny that a million times that would barely outweigh a paper clip. Within a minute, enough antimatter had been made which if exposed to regular matter would cause an explosion more powerful than five metric tons of TNT.

Within the day, that explosion would be more powerful than a small nuclear bomb.

But in that moment as Anak watched the main screen, he raised his hand with a flourish. "Ladies and Gentlemen, to the future!"

"To the future!" the team replied as one.

To the joy of everyone, the party food in the cafeteria was real and not the rations which they had been eating since the facility was sealed off. There was tender synth-sirloin, ice cream made by milking actual cows, mashed potatoes grown from the facilities' own hydroponics, and, of course, a cake designed in the shape of a synchrotron.

Dr. Samson was playing her violin while accompanied by Dr. Herbert on a grand piano. Not a single genius among them could explain how he smuggled *that* in. Anak didn't inquire, as anything that kept people from going insane in this cramped, underground facility was not something he was willing to condemn even on the principle of the thing. Besides, they were both talented musicians, and he sat back and tried to listen.

The party felt muted to Anak. There was all the reason to enjoy oneself, but for some reason he could not. Since he was thirteen, he had worked exclusively on this project, and now it was finished. The only thing left was maintenance.

"Are you enjoying the synth-sirloin, sir?" asked Dr. Helen, the vice-director, sitting across the table from Anak. She was a short woman, particularly from Anak's perspective, with short brown hair and thin eyebrows. Her intellectual stature, on the other hand, was anything but short. Her ability to wrangle personalities which could not be tolerated anywhere outside of academia had proven vital on any number of occasions, particularly in here, where tempers grew and the bonds of friendship broke.

"Yes," Anak said, idling toying with his

fork. "I will have to complement whoever programmed the robots."

"I wish Dr. Johnson had lived to see this," Dr. Helen said. Dr. Johnson's senseless death from falling off the ladder had impacted the whole staff.

Anak nodded.

"Well, Omnipotence chose to withdraw him from this world. Who are we to argue?" Dr. Helen asked. A silence fell between them, each lost in their own thoughts.

It was from Mr. Smith that Anak at age three first learned of death, and for that matter, of Omnipotence.

Washington Abraham Smith was one of the few surviving Survivors of Earth. He had been only a nine-year-old boy when the Final War began, ten when the Ixotak arrived too late to stop it. Decades later, he was now a hunched, wrinkled old man with long gray hair and blue eyes. His skin boasted more than a few scars, and one across his brow that he refused to explain.

Mr. Smith had been hired in his old age to share firsthand stories of Earth to the new princes and princess. He told them of grass and trees and birds and dirt. He told of rooms that stood alone and were called Buildings and invisible hallways between them called

Roads, because then the outside air was breathable and pleasant.

Being too publicly known and too well placed to fire or discipline, he did what he pleased, calling the immortal children by nicknames to the scandal of the other servants, and on one occasion, spanking a squirming princeling. Anak loved him like a favorite uncle, and Mr. Smith in turn called him "Big Boy."

They were in the play room as usual, a chamber full of toys and games of every kind and with more space than some citizens' entire suites. All the games had been turned off for classes, and almost all of the toys put away. Alexander could not be parted from his toy soldiers, and any servant who attempted this soon found their exposed appendages further exposed to Alexander's teeth. Out of fairness, the other two children were allowed a toy apiece. Anak had his favorite construction set, a number of atom models that fit together to make scientifically accurate chemicals. Anastasia had a picture book, the first one she had ever read. Mr. Smith sat on his chair watching them play and didn't mind as long as they listened to him wheeze through his stories.

The children had coaxed Mr. Smith that day into telling a story of the war's aftermath, a tragicomic tale involving a snake, a storm, a latrine, and his sister. "—and Pop spanked me three times," he said. "Once for letting her out, once because I got my good clothing ruined, and a third time because I didn't think to save the corpse for food. It got washed away in the rain. Carol got off free. Figure that one out."

"What does corpse mean?" Anak asked.

"It means what's left when something's dead, Big Boy. Where do you think meat comes from?"

Anastasia raised her hand, "It grows in vats."

"Not on Earth, it didn't, Know-it-all."

"What does dead mean?" Anak asked, still unsure about the whole concept of corpses.

"Dead means dead," Mr. Smith said. "Gone. Kaput. No more."

Alexander looked up from his armies. "It means it doesn't come back,"

"That's just it, Lil' Patton. It's gone for good."

Anastasia raised her hand again. "Where's your sister?"

"She's dead, too. Didn't make it through the winter. She's in Heaven now, I suppose."

"What's Heaven?" Anak asked.

Other servants quickly distanced themselves, lest the hidden cameras record their presence with any heresy that was about to be spoken. "Heaven is where God lives," Mr. Smith said. "Nowadays, everybody calls Him

Omnipotence because that's what the Ixotak call him, but back in my day we called Him God or the Lord and that was that."

"Who is God?" Anak asked.

"Awfully big question, Big Boy. But that's enough for today."

"Aw...," Anak said, and Alexander whooped for joy.

———◆———

"Yes, I suppose we can't argue with Omnipotence," Anak said after a pause. He wondered what Mr. Smith was doing now. They still exchanged messages from time to time, though that had dropped off in recent years. Of his batch-siblings, he was the only one to keep in touch with him. "One does wonder what Omnipotence thinks, sometimes."

Clearly uncomfortable, Dr. Helen changed the subject. "Do you think we can increase production, sir?"

"Aside from adding more reactors, you mean? I doubt it. We broke our backs trying to get to 0.1%, and I can't imagine that even the Ixotak have anything more efficient than we do. Despite their technology, they must obey the same laws of physics."

The explosion rocked the tables and sent the punch bowl rolling over its side and crashing into the ground where it shattered.

The piano stopped, and the violin squealed short. There was silence.

All eyes were on Anak. Both he and Dr. Helen reached for their tablets, and a second later the call came. "Your Immortal Highness, there was an explosion—" said the supervisor.

"We felt it," Anak interrupted. "What happened?"

"Trap Four lost power."

"Admiral Aizokek's five heads. Was anyone hurt?"

"Sir, we've lost contact with Dr. Bowyer," the supervisor said, her voice shaking.

There was a deeper silence.

"I told him he should have used a robot, but he wanted to look at the trap manually. Sir, there's no way he could have survived..."

"He's with Omnipotence now," Dr. Helen said in a hollow tone.

"Indeed," Anak said, and closed his eyes. Dr. Bowyer had been brilliant, if cavalier about safety. "Supervisor, send in a robot for the remains. And stop all accelerators," Anak ordered. "We *will* not lose any more people to stupid disasters like this."

"Yes, sir," the supervisor said.

"Do we have any idea why the trap lost power?"

"No, sir. The power was flickering, and then just winked out."

"Then we need to defuse the antimatter in

the other traps until we find out why." Anak looked up. "Dr. Ransom and Dr. Wolf, come with me. We need to defuse the remaining antimatter. Dr. Helen, set up a team to investigate."

"At once, sir," said Dr. Helen.

As Anak ran with the doctors and his guards to his office, he wondered about the magnitude of the lie with which mortals comforted themselves when one of them died. He had nothing against Dr. Bowyer himself. They were colleagues, if not friends, though friendship could hardly exist between mortal and immortal. Now that Dr. Bowyer was dead, friendship could never be. Anak did not believe in Heaven any more than he believed in the caring love of Omnipotence.

The day after he had learned of death from Mr. Smith, young Anak had one of his visits with his father. He had asked about Heaven.

He was sitting in his father's lap, playing with his atoms. His mother was playing a game with Anastasia and Alexander. Anak was uninterested, leaving him to spend time alone with his father.

"Pop," he began, "where is Heaven?"

"Heaven exists only in the imaginative minds of mortals who are unable to cope with their own mortality," replied "Pop." His voice was a kind tenor, as flowing and gentle as his long blond beard, and equally soft whether talking to his son or in solemn decree. "It is no more real than the games you play on the terminal."

This distinction was lost on Anak who was only three and believed everything was real. "But *where* is it?"

"Nowhere. It is nothing. There is no such place."

Anak fit a toy carbon to another toy carbon. "Then where does Omnipotence live?"

"Omnipotence lives nowhere. Omnipotence transcends the universe. Omnipotence is what we call Existence Itself, properly speaking *Ipsum Esse.* Only fools deny that Existence exists, but only greater fools believe Existence somehow cares about arbitrary groupings of matter and energy. The latter is a useful fable, and it behooves us to pretend to agree for political expedience. But do not be deluded, there is no Heaven."

Anak did not understand a word, as often happened in conversations with his father. "Then where is Carol?"

"Who?"

"Mr. Smith's sister. Mr. Smith said she was in Heaven."

"Mr. Smith is wrong. She no longer exists, any more than a toy that you've disassembled—

which you have done a distressing number of times."

"But Mr. Smith said—"

"Enough with Mr. Smith. He is a mortal; he cannot understand. You must think differently. You are immortal. "

"What does *that* mean?" Anak asked.

"You are a god among men. You will never die. But come. Enough of this morbid conversation." His father lifted him up, smiling. "Let us play."

———◇———

"I'm telling you, the substrate is at fault," Dr. Ransom said for the third time, his voice approaching a shout.

"And I'm telling you, that's impossible! It was a computer error!" Dr. Wolf said.

"Your continual bickering is nonproductive. Please concentrate on the matter at hand," Anak snapped.

"Sorry, sir," Dr. Ransom said.

"My apologies, sir," Dr. Wolf said.

They were in Anak's spacious office, cramped with him, his guards, and the doctors. Hardbound physics books from Newton to the latest speculations on the Ixotak's faster-than-light technology lined the bookshelves around the walls. Anak sat behind his wooden desk, clean except for a number of tablets. Before him Dr. Ransom and Dr. Wolf scribbled with their fingers on the main terminal.

Dr. Robert Grass Wolf, vice-director of Containment, was old and hunched over, mostly bald, and potbellied. He was always friendly, sometimes too much so, except for those whom he had grudges against. He had gotten his position by sheer seniority, if not for his accomplishment: he was on the team that made the first functional human general-purpose nanobots. He insisted on always wearing a lab coat over his bright blue jumpsuit of Tanihek's Arcolith.

Dr. Alec Rodney Ransom was in charge of the actual production of the Bowyer Traps. With a brown goatee and bloodshot eyes from working night and day, he looked more than a little like a stereotypical mad scientist. He was a high-ranking mortal from Anak's own arcolith. His pride in his social class produced no end of ire between him and his coworkers.

Anak sighed and held his head. "Look, let's review the basics. We know something went wrong. Our only question is what to do until we find it out and can prevent it from going wrong again."

"*If* it is a computer error, it could take days, weeks even to find out," Dr. Wolf said. "We're talking in the tens of thousands of lines to potentially debug just within the power control."

"We don't have days to leave what are practically several-ton antimatter bombs lying around in the vault," Anak said. "What if it's a flaw in the substrate?"

"Then no Bowyer Trap we have could be trusted. If Dr. Bowyer—he would've known exactly what to do, but..." Dr. Ransom stared off into the distance. "I can't believe he's gone."

"As difficult as Dr. Bowyer's loss is, our mission here is to prevent further tragedies," Anak said. "Until the investigative team gets back, there's no way for us to know what actually caused it. In either case, substrate or bug, we can't trust any antimatter storage we have whatsoever."

"Mhm," Dr. Ransom tapped on the main terminal a few times and brought up a strange design Anak had never seen before. "This is a defusing machine I designed. As you can see, you place a Bowyer Trap in this part. Ordinary matter is fed into this part, and it slowly annihilates the antimatter."

"Why wasn't I made aware of this machine earlier?" Anak asked. "This solves our problem."

"Sir, we'd lose the antimatter," Dr. Wolf said.

"We *don't* have a machine," Dr. Ransom said. "Dr. Bowyer—not to speak ill of the dead—said it was an unnecessary use of robot-time and materials."

Anak sighed again. Dr. Bowyer had also been arrogant. "How long would it take to make new machines of this type?"

Dr. Wolf gave the design a glare. "We'd have to test it first. We wouldn't want another accident."

"How dare you imply such a thing?" Dr. Ransom asked. "In all the simulations I ran—"

"I imply nothing. In all the simulations we ran, we never had an accident with the traps either."

"Disregarding the testing phase, how long would it take to build one?" Anak asked.

"We'd have to ask nanoengineering," Dr. Ransom said. "It's too complicated for the 3D printers."

"It is, but with my experience I'd say three hundred gram hours," Dr. Wolf replied, using the engineering terminology for the amount of work a gram of nanobots could accomplish in one hour.

"That long?" Anak asked. "How many grams of nanobots do we have? Three hundred?"

"It doesn't work that way, sir. It would take maybe a day, even with the most possible working nanobots. But I have a solution that will not take a day," Dr. Wolf said proudly.

"Go on," Anak said.

"Divide the remaining antimatter into small pieces, and transfer them to the other Bowyer Traps. We have more than enough traps that each trap will contain too little antimatter to explode."

"I object," Dr. Ransom said. "If the substrate is flawed, the same accident might happen while we're splitting up the antimatter."

"Yes, but no human would be close."

Anak thought for a moment. "This is what we will do: We will split up the antimatter as per your idea, Dr. Wolf, while we are waiting for the nanobots to construct Dr. Ransom's machine."

Dr. Ransom and Dr. Wolf looked at each other. "Of course, sir," Dr. Ransom said. "I'll begin construction immediately."

"I will supervise the redistribution, sir," Dr. Wolf said.

"Good. You are dismissed."

"Yes, sir," they both said.

Anak watched them bow and leave his office. As soon as they were gone he breathed deeply. In a few hours the antimatter would be safely divided. In a few days the problem would inevitably be found and solved, and production would resume. In a few months the incident would be just another of the few red marks on the facility's safety record.

But in all the years to come, there would be absolutely nothing Anak could do to bring Dr. Bowyer back into existence.

CHAPTER TWO

..the brief loss of power in Trap Four led to the explosion, killing Dr. Bowyer himself. We will all regret the loss of such an incredible mind. All personnel have been reminded that any dangerous activity must *be carried out by robots alone.*

Anak finished his report and transmitted a copy into the Immortal Family's archives. He encrypted the transmission by XORing it with a One Time Pad from a self-erasing chip, making a mathematically unbreakable ciphertext. Given the frequency of his reports, Anak was running out of pads. He made a mental note to obtain more pads from the archive's cryptography division when he was at home.

He appended the report to his personal research notes. These he encrypted onto his Immortal Family-issued tablet with a 4096-bit key. The key's size prevented anyone, the Ixotak included, from using brute force to decrypt it. The key itself was a selected section of his DNA. Every time he accessed his research, he had to prick himself with a special needle which read and decoded the necessary section. Finally, Anak locked the tablet in a small safe inside his desk.

The clock struck 1200. It was time. He got up and left for the lifts.

———◆———

As Anak and his guards approached the lift, he saw Dr. Helen inspecting the department heads who reported to her. Dr. Wolf in the bright blue full dress uniform of the Tanihek arcolith spoiled the effect by still wearing his slightly stained lab coat. His nemesis, Dr. Ransom adorned in Lauriel's lime green, reminded all gathered that he was related to the nobility. This irritated Dr. Erikson, the fusion reaction department head, who was also in Lauriel's lime green but with one less golden stripe. The Zozil Arcolith's black cape and cap swathing Dr. Bradley's huge girth was relieved only by crumbs caught in his beard. The Robotics department head was still crunching a nutrient bar. In contrast, the head physicist Dr. Fredrick, wearing the embroidered bright orange of Xem's Arcolith, resembled a child's picture book of extinct Earth animals. Only Dr. Samson, in her gold-trimmed black robes of Rororo's Arcolith, looked as sharp as the fine mind which made her the head of accelerators.

As the lift took the party up to the surface, Dr. Helen reminded her subordinates,

"An audience with the Immortal Family is a unique honor. Please follow the proper protocol as outlined in my memo to each of you."

"Pardon me, but we have already met royalty," Dr. Fredrick said. "Director Eloi is with us, after all."

"Do not presume familiarity with any other immortal or me," Anak said. "My family is not tolerant of obnoxious mortals."

"Of course, sir," Dr. Fredrick said, his eyes downcast.

The lift stopped, and the doors opened to the clear plexiglass dome that served as the exit to the facility. Both suns were shining outside; something primal within Anak wanted to go out and play. Yet his mind knew the poisonousness of the atmosphere could brew a dangerous storm at any moment, and the urge was easily repulsed.

Together, they walked through the corridor to the small tiltrotor waiting outside the dome. The interior was luxurious for an aircraft and included a touch and voice activated terminal, several comfortable seats, and a refrigerator holding real food. Anak strapped himself in by a window seat. "Please, make yourselves comfortable, sirs and ma'ams," said the steward. The others complied, and Dr. Bradley immediately went to the fridge.

When all were ready, Anak called for the pilot to launch. He watched the outside as the tiltrotor lifted off like a helicopter, then, as per its name, tilted its rotors to become a plane.

A few minutes later, Anak had the opportunity to see the arcoliths from above. Colossal with mirrored sides reflecting the sunslight, they were so huge that Anak's eyes played tricks on him, seeing as small and nearby what was far and gigantic. The arcoliths were laid out on a square grid equidistant from each other. The grid itself resided in the Great Crater, a huge ancient impact crater. Xenologists had speculated on how this arrangement was selected by the ineffable logic of the Ixotak. How the human society evolved in this unusual arrangement was even stranger.

As if by a physical law and not by human will, four neo-nations had formed, each in a corner of the grid: the Union of Alpha, the Automatocracy of Royale, the Obsidian League, and Anak's home, the Lauriel Genetic Federation. Each had gained control of its nearest neighbors, leaving only Aizokek's Arcolith in the center as neutral. Though peace treaties had been formed, tensions had been rising among them as if they were inevitably destined to fight for control of this small world.

Anak did not believe in inevitable destiny. Nor did he believe in those so-called sciences that prophesied that human nature was subjected to laws. He did not subscribe to the theory that advances in technology would one day allow scientists to predict the movements of nations as they did of atoms. The Ixotak had told humanity in their *Address at Landing on Refuge* that humans' own free will was culpable for what had happened. Like the Ixotak, Anak felt that if there was free will, humans themselves determined the course of their lives, not Nature.

His view was unorthodox among scientists, but it was his view.

The tiltrotor tilted again. Descending vertically, it hovered over a transparent dome on the top of Lauriel's Arcolith. The dome irised to let the tiltrotor land inside the arcolith. After the tiltrotor landed, the dome pumped Refuge's atmosphere out and an Earth-like atmosphere in. Anak unstrapped himself and prepared to enter his home.

———◆———

King Oberon Gustav Eloi VIIc5 looked the same as he did in Anak's earliest memories.

He was a tall wide-chested man with piercing lime-green eyes. In one hand he held a scepter made of a solid synthetic emerald, matching his great green fur robes. On his head he bore the Crown of Immortality, studded with emeralds and actual pearls.

Accompanied by five guards in green livery, all unfamiliar faces, King Oberon entered the dome just as Anak climbed down the stairs out of the tiltrotor. "Father!" Anak said, and they quickly embraced.

"Anak!" cried a familiar voice, and Anak found himself squeezed by Princess Anastasia too. She had grown significantly since he last saw her, Anak noticed, and her blond hair fell beneath her waist. She, too, wore a royal circlet and green fur robes. "How have you been? It's been so long."

"I've been doing just fine," Anak said, though remembering the death of Dr. Bowyer, that was not quite how he felt.

Anak's colleagues descended from the tiltrotor and knelt before the immortals.

"You may rise," King Oberon said.

"Father, may I present my staff," Anak said.

"My congratulations on your achievement," King Oberon said. "I also wish to express my condolences on the loss of your friend and colleague, Dr. Bowyer."

"Thank you, Father," Anak said.

"Let us be moving along then," King Oberon said.

They followed the king into the turbolift. Anak was silently thankful that there was enough room for all of them inside, particularly with Dr. Bradley.

"Floor 3021," King Oberon ordered, and the turbolift obeyed.

"We're going to the Palace Floor?" Dr. Erikson asked in a squeak.

"Of course," King Oberon said, before Anak could answer. "That is where the secure conference rooms are."

"But there's some artwork from Lost Earth there!" Dr. Erikson said, adding a quick "Sire."

"We are well aware of what exists in our own home," King Oberon said, and Anak winced. "You may admire it after the meeting is over."

"Oh. Thank you, sire."

The turbolift stopped, and they walked out into the guard station. The immortals passed through with only bows from the guards, while the mortals were stopped to be searched with sonic scanners. The king went on ahead, heedless of the delay, and Anak and Anastasia followed.

Luxury failed to describe the palace. No expense had been too much to honor the Immortal Family. The furniture was made of real, living wood, genetically engineered to shape itself. Each piece was a unique species. The rugs were green fur. Chandeliers of gold and emeralds hung from the ceiling, lit by beeswax candles. The priceless art from Lost Earth hung beside modern originals. Servants were everywhere in their green-and-gold tunics, dusting, cleaning, watering, bowing to greet the returning immortals.

"Father?" Anak said, as King Oberon paused to admire an aquarium of live fish, the LGF flag on their scales. "We should probably have left a guide for my staff."

"Oh, yes," King Oberon said, and snapped his fingers. "You! Guide the party from Facility 3-F to the conference room."

"Yes, sire," the servant said, and bowed.

The expansive conference room was as ornate as the rest of the palace. Hanging on the walls were genuine tapestries embroidered with the story of the founding of the Immortal Family. The wooden conference table gleamed with polish, at the head of which was positioned a small throne. The conferees' places each sported an ergonomic chair with a built-in terminal. Opposite the king's throne, a huge holoprojector created a scene of a forested river valley.

King Oberon had taken the throne already when the mortals arrived. "You may be seated," he said after they had genuflected to him.

Anak aimed his tablet at the holoprojector,

and the river valley dissolved into a three dimensional image of Facility 3-F.

"Our antimatter factory is now complete," Anak said. "It produces approximately one gram of antihydrogen a day. All the machinery is replicated five times and designed to operate in parallel, so that we are technically filling five Bowyer Traps at once. Actual production may vary due to maintenance of the various parts—"

"Excuse me," King Oberon interrupted. "I do believe production has halted recently?"

"It has indeed. There was an explosion. Dr. Ransom, if you will?"

"Yes, sir." Dr. Ransom walked up to the projector and cleared his throat. "I am Dr. Ransom, Ph.D in nanoengineering. I am also vice-subdirector of the containment department. After the explosion, I was assigned to the forensics team—"

Oh please, thought Anak, *talk about something other than yourself.*

"—where I worked on discovering what exactly happened. This is our current theory." Dr. Ransom tapped his tablet a few times, and the holoprojector displayed the image of a Bowyer Trap. "As you can see, the antimatter is held in magnetic suspension by room-temperature superconducting magnets. A flaw in the molecular substrate of the superconductor caused it to lose power, which led to a 'crack' in the magnetic bottle, which led to the antimatter escaping, subsequently exploding."

"Why was the substrate flawed?" King Oberon asked.

"Nanobot construction is an unsure thing, sire. The instructions are only *probably* obeyed, not necessarily correctly. Because production was rushed—"

"Pardon, Your Immortal Majesty, but the substrate failure was only one of several theories proposed," Dr. Wolf interrupted. "A computer error was likely the culprit."

"An error for which we have found no evidence?" Dr. Ransom asked. "One that conveniently absolves you of everything?"

"How dare you accuse me of such a thing?"

"I do dare accuse you, especially considering that—"

"Who are you?" King Oberon asked, turning to Dr. Wolf.

"I am Dr. Wolf, *the* Dr. Wolf, Ph.D in nanoengineering, and *the* subdirector of the containment department. My colleague must blame me for everything that goes wrong,"

"Not everything, only most of it," Dr. Ransom said.

"See! He even admits it!"

"I did not!"

"Oh yes you did! Did you not just say—"

Anak held his head and desperately wished he could be somewhere else.

Dr. Helen stood up and glared at the quarreling scientists, halting their argument. "My apologies, Your Immortal Majesty, for this display," she said. "Director Eloi is conducting a thorough investigation. While the exact cause has yet to be determined, production has been halted until safety can be guaranteed."

"A wise precaution," King Oberon said. "Might it be possible to increase production to make up for lost time?"

"Unfortunately not," Anak said. "The machinery is already pushed to the limit."

"Suppose an additional reactor was added?"

"Dr. Erikson?" Anak motioned to him.

Dr. Erikson stood. "Your Immortal Majesty, though it would be technically possible, it would require billions more credits. The facility is not designed with more than five reactors in mind. The coolant systems, for instance, are not able to handle six reactors, and are barely able to handle five. We've already had no end of trouble with them."

"We see," King Oberon said. "We suppose the next time we order the construction of an antimatter factory, we will specify the design to be more extensible. Do continue production at maximum speed whenever it is possible."

"Yes, Father," Anak said.

The meeting ended three hours later. When the mortals had left, Anak lingered to talk with his father.

"Father. I'm sorry about that argument," Anak said. "I—"

"Nonsense," King Oberon said. "Mortals are mortals. Their time is so short; every little thing seems precious to them. Thus they are constantly in conflict over the most trivial matters. Ironically, these conflicts only reduce their own lifespans."

Anak nodded. "Of course, Father. But we, on the other hand..."

"We need never disagree, because we are immortals. Every possession, every argument, everything to which mortals cling, will pass away, but we shall remain, forever."

"And speaking of perishable things," Anak said. "When's supper?"

"Two hours," Anastasia said without glancing at a clock. "If you're a little hungry, let's have some tea in the Earth room."

"I will leave you to that, then," King Oberon said. "I have another meeting."

The Earth room was a mostly accurate reconstruction of a wooden pavilion on Earth, complete with interactive walls simulating the clouds in the sky and the trees of a forest. It was only mostly accurate, Anak knew. Mr. Smith had said it was inaccurate, and he had refused to enter in on principle. There were, admittedly, known uses of artistic license. The "sun" was not bright enough to blind, nor did it produce ultraviolet rays. It never rained or snowed. The temperature was always pleasant, and there was no wind. The illusion was additionally damaged by anyone who came in or out of the doors, which though disguised when closed were obvious when open. But it was close enough for anyone born on Refuge.

Anastasia had revived the concept of tea from the books of Lost Earth. She had even discovered and translated a recipe for biscuits, which the servants had faithfully followed to the letter. Having popularized the idea among the upper classes, she ran a small tea business in her spare time, making a relatively small profit—compared to the finances of the rest of the Immortal Family. But the business was more for the enjoyment, Anastasia had explained, and besides, she simply enjoyed tea itself.

Anak was not quite so enthusiastic about sipping water mixed with boiled plant matter out of small ceramic vessels, but Anastasia was insistent. And, besides, it was a way to spend time with his batch-sister,

"I've read your reports, but I'm still wondering. What is antimatter, anyway?" Anastasia asked.

"Do you want the long physicist answer or the short layman answer?" Anak asked.

"What's the short answer?"

"Antimatter is the twin of normal matter. An antiparticle has all the characteristics of a normal particle of the same kind. Except that in some ways such as the electrical charge, the property is reversed."

"What kind of properties?"

"Suppose you have a proton. It has a positive charge. Take a antiproton. It has a negative charge. Electrons are negative. Positrons, their antiparticle, are positive."

"And antimatter is explosive, right?"

"It is when you expose it to regular matter. When you touch a proton to an antiproton, their mass is turned into pure energy. Same thing with an electron to a positron, or a neutron to an antineutron. That is why storing it is so difficult, though admittedly, it's easier than making it."

Anastasia took a sip. "Why's it so hard to make?"

"Because it only appears when you convert energy into matter. The process is very wasteful. Our efficiency, as you know, is only 0.07%, and that's incredible. It takes us fifteen gigawatts worth of fusion reactors to produce one gram in twenty-four hours. That's the energy of exploding three and a half tons of TNT every second."

"Fascinating," Anastasia said. "Why make it at all then? You could just skip the antimatter part and use the fusion reactors."

"It's useless as a power source, but it's great as a method of power storage." Anak nibbled on a biscuit. He liked biscuits better than the tea. "It's what the Ixotak use to fuel their engines. We can tell by the gamma rays they produce."

"I see. So that's why we're making it, right? To build our own war carriers?"

Anak looked around. "Yes, and to help the Ixotak refuel, but let's not talk of classified material. You never know who's listening."

"Yeah, sorry. Speaking of non-classified things, what's the status on FTL?" Anastasia's interest in the Ixotak's seemingly impossible faster-than-light travel had not abated since when she was young.

"Still no definite answers, and the Ixotak are recalcitrant as ever. I guess that's hardly news, sorry. There was a paper that might disprove the variable-c theory, but it's still under debate."

"Hmm. Well, I guess we'll find out one day."

"I know. With our unlimited lifespan, we'll live long enough to learn everything," Anak said.

"I don't know if we can learn *everything*," Anastasia said. "There's more books out there than I could possibly read."

"You still remembering everything you read?"

"Yes. In fact, Princess Cleopatra has been having me read even more recently. I've lost count of how many reports I've read."

"Well, just tell yourself the job's temporary. It is, isn't it?"

"So Father tells me. I can't imagine what he wants me do to after this."

"Well, you're bound to like it. See how happy Alex is. Speaking of him—"

A servant entered through the doors and bowed. "Prince Anak? Your flight is ready."

"Sorry, have to go," Anak said, standing up. He stuffed down another biscuit.

"It's okay," Anastasia said. "I have work, too."

"See you later then. Take care!"

"You too!"

CHAPTER THREE

ANAK WOKE UP SCREAMING.

He groaned and felt his beating heart and sweat-stained fur blankets. It was the nightmare again. As vivid as it was, and as often as it recurred, he could remember few details. Why, by the Ixotak's valor, it always started with a minature golf course was beyond him. Though, he supposed it made as much sense as the rest of it. He was always about to swing when the evacuation alarm went off. He'd run down the corridor to find that the lifts didn't work. While pounding on the control panel, he'd feel an icy touch on his shoulder. He would turn and see Dr. Bowyer's charred corpse had come back to life, grinning. And then he would scream himself awake.

It was all illogical, of course. The lifts were designed, in case of an evacuation, to get Anak out first. Though he had had to see Dr. Bowyer's corpse, he had also seen the body cremated. And there was no room in the facility for something as frivolous as a golf course. Then again, trying to dissect a dream in terms of logic was like discovering exactly how the horse had escaped from the barn before locking it shut.

It was the ninth such nightmare in the three months since Dr. Bowyer's funeral. He wondered what was so upsetting to him that he kept having it. Was it the arbitrariness of the death? No, Dr. Johnson's tragic fall from the ladder had been pointless, and yet he had never dreamed of being chased up a ladder. Guilt, then? True, he was responsible for whatever happened in this facility, accidental or not. But then again, they were accidents, caused by people ignoring the safety protocols.

Perhaps it was that what happened to Dr. Bowyer could just as easily have happened to himself. That, immortal or mortal, he would be just as dead.

———◆———

His memory of learning the fact of his mortality was almost perfect, as if it had burned itself like a brand into his nervous tissue.

It was at ten that Anak had discovered the wonders of the arconet. While his tablet had filters, the last technician to perform maintenance on Anak's tablet was easily bored and had removed them in order to surf while he waited. He was also forgetful and forgot to remove access when he was done. (Anak had learned how it had happened later when the technician was demoted to the lowest class for his crimes.)

While Anak was doing his homework in his magnificent bedroom, he looked up the meaning of the Ixotak word-star Hek. The search results, rather than being blocked out except for the necessary dictionary entry, lead to a poorly made Ixotak-Human translator.

Curious, he input his entire homework question in, only to receive a passable answer: *Warriors of Omnipotence, sleep not.* His curiosity turned to delight as he began to rush through the rest of his homework, exchanging time spent straining his brain over the Ixotak's five-fold poetry for time to play with his tablet. Further delight came as he explored other forbidden terms. He typed in his own name.

"Anak Og Eloi XIa11 is a child of the eleventh generation of the Immortal Family..." He tapped on another link. "Immortal Family. n. The ruling body of the Lauriel Arcolith and the whole Lauriel Genetic Federation. Currently there are five living generations, or batches..." Anak knew something was wrong at that point, but he continued tapping.

"...the batch number of an immortal refers to which batch they were produced in (see, cloning batches). VIIc5, in King Oberon's name, refers to being of the seventh batch, section c, zygote five."

Anak typed in "first batch".

It was not a page, but a subsection. "... none of the first batch of the Immortal Family survived beyond birth, though the cells were proven to be clinically immortal..."

Anak tapped immortal. "Clinical Immortality. n. The state of being ageless. Clinical immortality in modern times refers to *Homo* and *Sylvilagus immortalis,* the two vertebrate immortal species. Clinical immortality does not prevent death by other means..."

The last line was immediately italicized by Anak's mind. *"Does not prevent death by other means."*

He stared at those words. Surely, surely it was a mistake. His father had said he was immortal. He couldn't die. He *couldn't* die. His life was eternal, wasn't it? His very genes told him this. It was decreed since birth that he was an immortal god.

But it all made such horrible sense. Why did they have guards and self-defense training? Why did they have food tasters? Why did they have doctors? Why did Father forbid Anastasia from trying to construct a Tesla coil, saying it was too dangerous? Why any of these things, unless they were as fragile as those they ruled?

"Prince Anak?" called a servant. "It's time for Mr. Smith's class."

Anak quickly hid his tablet and followed the servant into the play room.

The children were older now, and Mr. Smith as well. Anastasia no longer carried her picture book around, and Alexander had progressed to more virtual battles. Mr. Smith was now wheelchair bound.

"What's wrong, Big Boy?" asked Mr. Smith.

"Nothing," said Anak, sitting down.

"Yeah, right, it's nothing. You shouldn't tell a lie."

This piece of advice had long since been intercepted by a more Machiavellian notion from his father, but Anak still could not lie to Mr. Smith. "I, um, err..."

"What? Spit it out."

"I could die. I'm—I'm not really immortal."

Anastasia and Alexander gave Anak the most curious look, the servants turned pale, and Mr. Smith blinked.

"'Course you're not," Mr. Smith said. "Everything dies. I don't know about all this 'Immortality' nonsense y'all talk about."

"But—But—"

"None of that. It's the way things are. There's no use pouting about it."

"But I don't want to die!" Anak screamed, the last word extended until his breath ran out and his lungs hurt. He began to cry.

"No one wants to die," Mr. Smith said. "You'll just have to live with it,"

"No! No! No!"

King Oberon rushed into the room with his guards. "Anak, my son, what is wrong?"

"I—I—" Anak could not get the words out. "I—I—"

"Your son just learned what 'clinical' in clinical immortality means," Mr. Smith said.

For the first time in Anak's life, he heard his father angry. "How dare you, mortal," he hissed.

"I didn't tell him, he found out himself, somehow."

King Oberon knelt by Anak's side and hugged him. The warmth of his father could not comfort Anak. "Anak, Anak, where did you learn this?"

It was several moments before he could string together the words. "The—the tablet t—t—old me."

"You shouldn't've hid it from him," Mr. Smith said. "It's not right, tricking him into thinking he's a god, when he's not."

"Silence, mortal!" King Oberon shouted, and then turned back to Anak. "Anak, my son, it is all right."

"No, it isn't! Not if I can die!"

"Hush!" He stroked Anak's head. "Your life is safe, safer every day. One day, the danger will be so close to zero that it will no longer be worth even considering. One day, we will all be truly immortal."

"Really?" Anak asked.

"Really," King Oberon said.

"Not really," Mr. Smith said. "It's all a load of baloney."

"George Washington Smith, I will tolerate no more of this," King Oberon said.

"I won't tolerate it, either. You're raising these kids to believe a lie, and I won't go along with it." Mr. Smith folded his arms and scowled.

"Very well then," King Oberon said, standing up to his full height. He motioned to a guard. "Please escort Mr. Smith from the Palace Floor."

The guard saluted and took the handles of the wheelchair. "And the serpent said to Eve, 'Ye shall be as gods'..." Mr. Smith called out behind him as the guard wheeled him out.

"Can we really die?" Anastasia asked, looking up to her father.

"Not if all the powers and force of the Lauriel Genetic Federation can help it," King Oberon said. "Fear not, your lives are secure."

"But we can still die," Anak said, in between sniffs.

"Do not let that old mortal taint your thinking. There is no point worrying about death. You are as immortal as immortal can be. You need only wait and work, and you will become truly immortal."

———◆———

That had been the last time Anak had seen Mr. Smith in person though he had secretly continued contact through the mail. Though, on further thought, his father probably knew about that, too.

He checked the clock in his room. 0700. Two hours before he was supposed to be awake.

He supposed he could check the news. It was one of the few things that was allowed to come from outside. He reached for his tablet on his nightstand and woke it from sleep. He checked the headlines.

"Union Denies Construction of Nukes." "The Ixotak War Carrier *The Colorful Dust of Stars* in System, Three New Craters On Surface, Say Xenologists." "King Oberon to Give Speech Tonight, Announce Names of New Immortal Batch." "Pope Sixtus VI Condemns Rivalry Between Neo-Nations." "Survivor of Earth Near Death."

The tablet fell from Anak's frozen hands.

It was as he feared: "George Washington Smith, the oldest remaining Survivor of Earth, collapsed from a heart attack today. He is currently in critical condition at Lauriel's Arcolith, Floor 1562. Doctors say—"

No.

No.

NO!

———◆———

He wandered the facility in a daze, haunted not by a nightmare but by his own thoughts. His guards followed, silent.

He knew Mr. Smith was mortal, that one day he would die as would all of his obsolete species. He knew this, but could not believe it. Mr. Smith had been a fixture of his childhood. And now, he would soon be gone forever?

No. He would not accept this. He *could* not accept this. There had to be some way, some technique, some experimental surgery that would prolong Mr. Smith's life. Prolong it long enough, and perhaps a cure for all mortality could be found for him.

Perhaps the Ixotak would have some godlike power to save him. Their technology was powerful beyond what humans knew. Perhaps they had medical nanobots more sophisticated than any humans could produce that could reassemble his body, repair his heart. Perhaps they had a formula to put him in some kind of cryostasis. For all he knew they had brain-uploaders to put Mr. Smith's mind on a computer.

If nothing else, Anak knew they could send Mr. Smith to the nearest black hole, where the warped fabric of space-time would slow down time from his perspective, until the day they found a cure. There was even a war carrier in system, perhaps—

But, no. Perhaps the Ixotak could do these things, but how could he ask even one of them to abandon their mission to save a single human? Unless they had a panacea for every human ill, one that they had refused to give despite every human pleading, there was no hope to be had from the Ixotak.

No, Anak knew he would have to face this, the same way that he faced the deaths of Dr. Bowyer and Dr. Johnson and all his other dead colleagues. He would have to face the fact that living as an immortal among mortals, all his mortal acquaintances would one day pass on, and he would remain.

Although there had been no time to say goodbye to his lost colleagues, Anak had at least seen them every day. Mr. Smith would die alone in some hospital bed far away. Anak needed desperately to see him one last time, to assure himself that there was no way to prevent his death.

Yet, how could Anak justify leaving the facility? The king had not allowed Dr. Samson even to contact her dying mother. He certainly would not allow Anak, the facility director, to leave on behalf of a mortal despised by His Immortal Majesty.

No. There must be some way Anak could

see Mr. Smith one final time. Then it struck Anak. The One Time Pads. Only immortals were allowed access to the archive vault where they were stored. In his rush to make his flight, he had forgotten to get more of them. He had the perfect excuse to leave the facility. All he needed was to come home for the pads, and he could arrange to visit Mr. Smith for the last time.

CHAPTER FOUR

THE TRIP WAS DELAYED AN additional day due to storms, and Anak cursed the weather.

King Oberon was waiting for him the moment the tiltrotor landed. "Hello, my son," he said, handing him a small case. "Inside are all the pads you will need for the next, oh, five years?"

"Thank you, Father," said Anak, taking the case. He moved to go past, but the king stretched out his arm.

"Aren't you going to leave, now?" King Oberon asked.

Anak stumbled for words. "I have some other important business—"

King Oberon motioned him to come along. "Please. I am not an idiot. I have reviewed all your reports. What business could you possibly have? You have ulterior motives to come here, or you would have asked a cousin to bring the pads to you. Explain."

"Father," Anak realized there was no use hiding it. "Mr. Smith is dying."

"I had heard. And what did exactly did you plan on doing? Wave a magic wand over his shriveled body to renew it? Perhaps develop an elixir of eternal youth?" He motioned the turbolift open.

"I planned on seeing him," Anak said as they stepped inside. "Before... before he's gone."

"He is a mortal. Are you planning on visiting *every* mortal's deathbed?"

"Mr. Smith is a friend."

"Why?" King Oberon asked, and said to the elevator, "Floor 3021."

"Why not?"

"You have nothing in common, my son. He is a mortal; you are immortal. He is a Morlock; you are Eloi. You have no reason to be friends."

"Father, this isn't about reason," Anak said.

"Excuse me?" King Oberon asked.

"Father, you are not my real father. Technically speaking, you and I both were genetically engineered from scratch. We share no blood except for the Eloi genes."

"Nonsense. I am your father in every way that matters."

"And what matters?" Anak asked. "That I think of you as kin, so that I will love you?" The lift stopped, and they emerged into the guard room. The guards knelt, and the king

49

walked on with Anak. "That I live like your child, so that I will listen to you?"

"Yes, what of it?"

"Neither of those things are rational. It has everything to do with our emotions and instincts. So when my instincts tell me to see Mr. Smith, what is wrong with that?"

"My son, if you let yourself become attached to mortals, you will only destine yourself to heartbreak."

"But Father, what further harm can it do? I'm already attached to Mr. Smith, and nothing except his death will break that bond."

"Then let him die!" Anak heard the rare note of anger in his father's voice. "Break that bond! Do not let yourself become enslaved to your own emotions!"

"I will not let myself become enslaved. Except..."

"Except that you already are?"

"Except this is the last time, the very last time. After this, I will no longer become attached to any mortal." Anak thought of his colleagues, those he had labored with for the past three years. Those relationships were strictly professional. He could remain unattached.

King Oberon nodded. "If you insist. Very well, you have convinced me. Go, and see George Washington Smith. But do not return for any mortal, ever again."

"I will not," Anak said. "I will not."

———◆———

"I'm sorry, sir," said the mortal clerk in the politest yet least regretful tone. "Mr. Smith is unavailable for visitors."

"What?" Anak's worried frown became a scowl.

"He has given explicit orders not to be disturbed."

"But—Do you know who I am?"

"I am sorry, sir, but I cannot help you,"

"But—"

But the clerk returned to her terminal screen.

This sight infuriated the already irate Anak, whose mind flashed through several extremely stupid but satistifying courses of action, such as smashing his fist through the glass screen. Then several more possible but futile courses of action, such as threats and bribes of class merits and demerits. No, he was better than those ideas, and mortals were watching. At last he said, "Ahem,"

The clerk looked up. "Yes, sir?"

"Tell him—tell him Big Boy came to see him."

"As you wish, sir."

Anak returned to his seat, and his guards followed, one to either side.

Several minutes later, which felt like a small eternity, a nurse in pale green scrubs emerged and said, "Your Immortal Highness? Mr. Smith wants to see you."

Anak followed the nurse down the hallways of the hospice. He smelled antiseptics and death. They stopped outside Mr. Smith's room. The nurse poked a head inside and said, "Please wait."

Anak waited, and after she nodded, stepped inside the curtain.

When he saw Mr. Smith, Anak felt like his heart was going to burst. Mr. Smith was so yellowed and wrinkled that Anak thought he was dead at first. The old man's lids barely opened to see Anak. "Hey, Big Boy. Haven't seen you in a while."

"Nor I, you," Anak said.

"How's it going? How big are you, now, anyway?"

"I am one point eighty-five meters tall."

"In real numbers, I mean."

Of all the things Anak thought he might discuss at a death bed, obsolete systems of measurement were not among them. "I... don't really know. Mr. Smith?"

"Yes?"

Anak took a chair and moved it to the bedside. "I'm... I'm sorry. I should have come sooner, but—"

"Don't apologize, Big Boy. We all have to die someday. Even you."

Anak wiped his eyes, finding them blurred by tears. "I, I don't know what to say."

"Don't say anything then, just sit by me," Mr. Smith said. "Just sit by me."

———◆———

Anak must have sat there for hours for when the nurses came to wheel Mr. Smith out to another test, Anak was famished. ("Can't you just leave me in peace?" Mr. Smith had asked. "What're you going to find out? That I'm dying?")

A doctor came by as Anak waited outside in the hallway, and Anak asked only one question. "Is there absolutely nothing you can do?"

"Nothing, Your Immortal Highness," the doctor said. "His heart has simply worn out. I am sorry to say, sir, but short of a miracle there is no way he will live. And even if he did, he has reached the end of his natural lifespan. I understand it may be difficult for an immortal such as yourself to comprehend—"

"You understand nothing," Anak snapped. "I know full well what it means to die."

The doctor winced as if struck. "I am sorry, sir. I misspoke. I merely wished to say that situations like these are why *Homo immortalis* was created in the first place."

"Of course," Anak said and regretted his earlier words. He should be more composed than that. But, there was no apologizing to a mortal. He was hungry and upset, that was all. He turned to his guards. "I desire food. We will go to the cafeteria."

"Sir," said one guard. "The cafeteria food is not cleared for your safety. Perhaps you wish to have food sent in?"

Anak thought. He was tired of the place, and Mr. Smith would not be back for some time. "No. On second thought, I will go to the Palace Floor to eat."

"Of course, sir."

———◊———

Anak ate at the dinner table in silence. The food was beyond excellent, prepared by the finest cooks. It also had the additional property of not being rations, which would have made Anak dance for joy normally. But there was no forgetting what was happening.

Anastasia nudged Anak. "What's wrong?" she whispered.

"Mr. Smith is dying," he whispered back.

Anastasia was silent.

Anak looked around. Of the twelve immortals there, only he and Anastasia had had a significant relationship with a mortal. Although she was fond of Mr. Smith, only Anak had remained in touch. How could she and the others understand what he was going through?

"My children," King Oberon said. "Please concentrate on your meal and not on whispering to each other. Is there something I need to know?"

"Sorry, Father, I'm just thinking."

"Relationships with mortals are prohibited for good reasons," Queen Titania said, as if reading his thoughts. "It only leads to suffering."

Anak thought of saying something angrily, but then thought better of it. "Of course, Mother."

"Theoretically," Anastasia said. "Couldn't we put him in a Rachel Stasis?"

There was quiet across the table. Anak asked, "What is a Rachel Stasis?"

"It's a technique developed by an anesthesiologist named Dr. Candace Lorenz Rachel. She researches hibernation in mammals. She's found a way to keep rabbits under a special kind of hibernation, for years even, and when they were revived, they remembered all their training."

Anak felt hope rising in his chest. "And you think she might be able to do it with humans, too?"

"She's already done it with humans. Thrill seekers, the elderly, the terminally ill. The technology is dangerous and expensive, though."

Neither of which matters, Anak thought.

We have enough funds to do anything, and Mr. Smith would die anyway. Of course, some of those funds weren't his. "How expensive?" Anak asked.

Princess Cleopatra cleared her throat, and said, in her usual neutral tone, "We are funding her research. Expense wouldn't be a factor."

"So then—" Anak began.

King Oberon stroked his beard. "You are sorely trying my patience on this matter."

"Father, he's a national treasure. Surely you cannot object—"

"Why would I object? If this method would preserve his life, then by all means do so. But please, reduce your hysterics the next time a mortal is dying."

"I understand, Father."

"Good."

———————◆———————

In the end, the only problem proved to be Mr. Smith's objection.

"No," he said.

"Pardon?" Anak wondered if he had explained the procedure properly.

"No means no, Big Boy." Mr. Smith shook his head, a slight movement barely perceptible. "I've already lived a full lifetime. I don't need to be 'immortal' like one of you kids."

Anak reached for an argument, and came up empty. "I—I, please."

"No."

"You could see Earth again, if you wanted," Anastasia said. "You'd still be around when the Ixotak return to take us home."

"It wouldn't be what I remembered. 'Sides, I wouldn't be able to do much but sit in a wheelchair and look around."

"Mr. Smith?" Anak asked.

"I'm listening. Ain't got much else left to do."

"This—this isn't so much about what you or I want. It's about doing what's right."

"What's right is for people to grow old and die, just as the Lord intended."

"No! Don't you see? You're the oldest Survivor. You're the last one who knew what it was like to live on Earth. Everyone else was just a toddler or less. Think of what it would mean to return to Earth with you. You'd be able to—to *make* it what you remembered. To return ourselves to the way things were before the Final War."

"There's books for that. You don't need me."

"But they need to hear it from your own mouth," Anastasia said. "Like we did, when we were kids,"

"Who would listen?"

"Children would. *My* children would, if I

ever have any," Anak said. Or ever could. It was a complicated matter.

"Well..."

"Please, Mr. Smith. I know you don't have anyone else left except us. Think of us as your grandchildren. If you have no other reason to live, live for us. Live for *me*."

Mr. Smith closed his eyes and breathed for several moments. Anak almost thought Mr. Smith had fallen asleep from the morphine again, when he said, "What's all involved in this treatment, anyway?"

"It'd just be like going to sleep," Anastasia said. "They'd put you under anesthesia, and then... Well, it gets more complicated."

"Will they be poking any new holes in me? Mind you, I've got enough as it is."

"No. I mean, maybe, but if they did it would be absolutely painless."

Mr. Smith closed his eyes again. "And I'd wake up back on Earth, you say."

"You would. It would just be an instant for you."

There was a painful pause. "No. It's not natural."

"Excuse me," said a plaintive voice. "Am I interrupting something? Oh, I'm sorry, Your Immortal Highnesses."

Anak turned to see a small young man in black with a white collar enter the room. Mr.

Smith looked up, and for the first time seemed genuinely alert. "You're the priest?"

"Yes. If you would rather I come at a different time."

"No, no, it's fine. I just expected someone, y'know, older. You know all that Latin stuff?"

"I do. You see, I was with the Sacred Order of Old Terra before they rejoined with Rome."

"What's all that?"

"Erm, never mind. I know the 'Latin stuff'."

Anak was genuinely surprised at the priest's presence. From Mr. Smith's letters Anak had assumed that he had rejected organized religion in all its forms. Well, mortals did strange things as the end of their existence approached.

Anak motioned to Anastasia, and they both stepped out. "Well, I tried," she said. "Maybe if Alex was here..."

"I don't think Alex ever liked Mr. Smith," Anak said. "But listen, I have a plan."

"We are going to be in *so* much trouble if Father finds out," Anastasia said for about the fourth time.

"And what exactly would he do to us?" Anak asked, looking over her shoulder at the terminal screen. "He wouldn't harm his precious children."

"I don't know, but I think he'd find

something," Anastasia answered. She tapped the screen a few times. "Are you sure there's no other way than this?"

"The Mortalists would throw a fit if they heard we were trying to override the decision of a mortal, especially a Survivor."

"They'll throw a bigger fit if we're caught."

"We won't be."

"Says the one who knows nothing about hacking," Anastasia glared at the screen for a moment and tapped a few more times. "All right, here we go."

To everyone outside the innermost circles of LGF, a handwritten signature could not be counterfeited. After all, when forensic handwriting specialists could use sophisticated algorithms to help detect the most advanced forgeries, how could forgers still succeed? However, what computers could help spot, computers could help fake. Anastasia's vast knowledge included a report on a signature duplication program. With her credentials, she had access both to the code and the mainframes required to run it.

They had already created the falsified form. At that was left was to add it to the chart. "Are you sure you want to do this?" Anastasia asked.

"We have to save him," Anak said. "He's not in his right mind. We're just doing the right thing."

"But we won't be making him immortal," Anastasia said.

"Not now, no. But one day. Think of how advanced nanobots have become. What if, one day, nanobots could repair everything that goes wrong, even old age? What if, one day, we crack the problem of consciousness and can make the dying into living computer programs? What if, one day, we find a way to add the Eloi genes into the DNA of mortals? There's no telling what future technology can do."

"And if it doesn't do any of those things?"

"We can still bring Mr. Smith to see Earth one last time." Anak said.

"You're right," Anastasia said and pressed the button.

———◊———

Ever since he could read, whenever Anak was worried, he researched. What he researched didn't matter, as long as it was interesting enough to take his mind off the problem. The off-hand reference by the young priest to the Sacred Order of Old Terra was enough for Anak to now, in this cramped waiting room with his tablet, to dive into the controversy.

"The Sacred Order of Old Terra was a sedevacantist sect that formed after the Council of Vatican II-Aizokek's Arcolith. They claimed that the cardinals known to have survived

61

the Final War and the Ixotak's Rescue were not the only surviving cardinals, and that the true successor to Pope John XXIII remained in exile on Earth (see: Earth Survival Conspiracy Theories). Rejecting the liturgical reforms of the Council, they were openly hostile to the Alien Theological and Neo-Roman movements. They were never a large group, and as time passed..."

Anak was amazed at how vehemently mortals could argue over things that neither mattered or even existed.

"...the main topic of the Council of Vatican II-Aizokek's Arcolith was whether the Son was Incarnated once for all races, or once in each race (see: xenophysite theology). No definite answer was reached, though the Council ruled that the question may be answerable in the future when more is known about the Ixotak..."

The wonder of learning new words, such as sedevacantist and xenophysite, took his mind off wondering what was happening to Mr. Smith right now. What if Mr. Smith had found out about Anak's deception? Anak, for some unknown reason, was still troubled over what he had done. But why should he be? He had done the right thing.

"Xenophysitism, sometimes called Polyphysitism, is the theological view that the Incarnation of the Son occurs once in every intelligent species. Thus, Christ would have

both a Human and Divine nature, but also an Ixotak nature. Xenophysitism is also the belief that there are separate Churches for every species. Critics often argue..."

Hours, or possibly minutes, later, Anak had lost track of time until a tall bald woman in a doctor's uniform entered the waiting room. "Your Immortal Highness?" she asked. "The treatment was successful."

Anak's heart leaped. "Thank you, Dr. Rachel. Would it be safe to see him?"

She hesitated for a moment. "No, sir. The containment unit must be kept absolutely sterile and unexposed to light. Even if you wished to put on scrubs, sir, you would not see anything, only a black, coffin-like container."

That description sounded unintentionally disturbing to Anak. "Very well, I will leave him in your hands."

"Yes, sir. We would do anything to preserve his life."

Anak turned to his guards. "We shall go."

He was silent as they walked back to the lifts, and from there to the tiltrotor domes.

It was only long after they had already taken flight that he allowed himself to cry.

CHAPTER FIVE

TEARS FADED INTO EMOTIONS, AND emotions into memories, until Anak no longer had to call every morning to make sure the stasis was successful. Anastasia was there in the arcolith in case anything happened, and unlike Anak she had time on her hands.

Anak, on the other hand, had the most boring, tedious, and unchallenging work imaginable.

The fusion reactors fused for power, the accelerators produced antimatter, the Bowyer Traps contained. The machinery worked without fault or cessation, except for maintenance. There were no more deaths. There were no further design problems to be solved; no more puzzles to conquer with his mind. Everything was going as well as possible.

With the lack of interesting work, Anak was in his office with one of his hobbies: translating some Ixotak poetry into Human. He was taking part in a volunteer project from Aizokek's Arcolith, with translators working together across the borders of arcoliths and even neo-nations. Anak had already translated a few to somewhat good reviews, though he was still improving.

This poem was from the Cultural Dump, that archive that the Ixotak had left shortly before they themselves left. There were few historical references, nor were there any references to the Foe, a well-known fact that puzzled xenologists to no end.

The poem in question—poem was inaccurate if technically correct, as all Ixotak "speech" was poetic, in the same way that all human speech contained hints of music—was by the Ixotak philosopher Gejitok. Anak's most recent translation went:

> Fear the fool who believes
> his nation, alone among all,
> will survive all time's erosion,
> and on the Final Day,
> speak to Omnipotence as equal.

Anak was deciding between "Fear" and "Beware" for the first line when the call came on the main terminal. He gestured for it to open, and Dr. Helen was on the other side. "Yes, Dr. Helen?"

Her face was concerned. "Director Eloi, we've got another problem. Dr. Ransom and Dr. Wolf are calling for each other's resignation."

"Do they have nothing better to do than pester each other?" Anak asked.

"Apparently not," Dr. Helen said with a strained laugh. "Both refuse to work with the other. In fact, Dr. Wolf told me he would resign unless we appoint a different vice-subdirector under him."

"Have them come to my office. You, too, please."

"Yes, sir."

"If either of you wish to begin like middle schoolers and accuse the other of 'starting' it, please do not waste your time," Anak said, before either could start. "I am absolutely tired of this idiotic vendetta you two have against each other. What has either of you done to deserve this?"

"What has he done? What has he done?" Dr. Ransom asked with laughter. "What *hasn't* he done?"

"Dr. Ransom is a plagiarist and a liar," Dr. Wolf said.

"What has he lied about?" Dr. Helen asked.

"Everything. He stole credit for my work," Dr. Wolf said.

"Your work? 'Your' work had more to do with my own labors than yourself," Dr. Ransom said.

"See? He's lying again!"

"I am not, you scoundrel."

"Scoundrel? There's one scoundrel in this room, and I am not the one."

"Stop," Anak said. "Just stop, or else—"

"Or else what?" Dr. Ransom asked. "What are you going to threaten us with? Expulsion from the facility? Believe me, I'd like nothing more than to leave this place for good. I'm tired of looking at the same old walls, eating the same rations in the same cafeteria, with absolutely nothing new or interesting to do. I want to go home. I want to *retire*."

"For once I must agree with Dr. Ransom," Dr. Wolf said. "Why do you not let us leave?"

"Classified," Anak said. "It's—"

"What *isn't* classified?" Dr. Ransom asked. "Let me put this out in simple terms, ones so simple that an arrogant overindulged sixteen-year-old prodigy can understand. I. Have. Had. Enough."

"I understand we are all stressed—" Anak said.

"I understand what we're really here for," Dr. Wolf interrupted. "It's to blow up arcoliths, isn't it? A nuke can get shot down, but nothing can stop an antimatter bullet. In fact, I can work out right now how fast the bullet would need to be, and how much antimatter it needs."

"That's ridiculous," Dr. Helen said. "Do

you think humanity has forgotten the lessons of the Final War?"

Anak shook his head. "Let us ignore all the innumerable reasons that antimatter weapons do not make sense. If that was the case, why do you think that would make me let you leave?"

"Because..." Dr. Wolf trailed off.

"I don't care if this is a weapons plant," Dr. Ransom said. "I don't care if you want to blow up arcoliths. I don't care even if you want to blow up the Ixotak. I just want to go home."

"Impossible. Even *I* cannot go home," Anak said.

"Oh, yeah? And what was that appearance in the news all about?" Dr. Wolf asked.

"A family emergency," Anak said.

"What kind of emergency?" Dr. Ransom demanded.

"A friend of mine was dying."

"And yet you did not let Dr. Sampson visit her mother, did you?" Dr. Wolf asked.

"That was my father's decision, not mine."

"Listen," Dr. Helen said. "This is all irrelevant. Will either of you reconsider your positions?"

"No," they said simultaneously, and then glared at each other.

"As it happens, we don't need much of the containment department, now that the design phase is finished," Anak said. "Take a break, both of you. Do something else for the next week or two, or however long it takes for you to stand each other."

"*I* can tolerate his shenanigans just fine," Dr. Ransom said. "*He* cannot tolerate me."

"On the contrary, it is you who—"

Anak groaned. "Stop. Just stop. I can't take it anymore. Go swim, or sing, or do whatever it is that you do in your spare time. Right now."

"I will do just that," Dr. Wolf said, and stomped out the door.

"If you insist," Dr. Ransom said, and left.

Anak turned to Dr. Helen. "What on Refuge convinced me to hire these two?"

Dr. Helen shrugged. "It was your decision, sir. They weren't always this bad."

———◆———

Anak couldn't sleep, wrapped in fur blankets on his massive bed.

Maybe it was the nightmares again. Maybe the rations had gone bad, and he was feeling sick to his stomach because of them. But maybe most, he thought, he was wondering about Dr. Wolf's words.

Were they building arcolith-killers? The concept was ridiculous, the arcoliths were practically invincible. Arcolite, what humans called the material that made them up, had resisted the sharpest cutters. Powerful lasers bounced off while barely warming it. Every attempt to even remove a piece had proven fruitless. A party of physicists, whose arguments Anak understood well, claimed that arcolite wasn't a true material, but the result of a kind of forcefield, the unknown Fifth Force. The counterargument was that the Ixotak's ships, also apparently made of arcolite, had battle scars, which made no sense if arcolite was the result of some kind of forcefield generator. Anak had taken neither side.

Then again, the orbital defense platforms would shoot down anything that flew too fast towards an arcolith, implying that there was something that could endanger them. Similarly, the very existence of battle scars proved that they could be injured. Surely if anything, antimatter could do it. Was Dr. Wolf right? Were they making antimatter bullets?

At last he decided to bring up a physics simulator on his tablet. There was no known values for the strength of arcolite, except for guesses based on architectural necessity. But he didn't need them. He only needed to see if an antimatter bullet was possible, and then he could go back to sleep.

He worked for about an hour, sleepless but alert. At last he came to the conclusion that Dr. Wolf was exaggerating. The very explosiveness of antimatter would cause it to disintegrate as it approached the side of the arcolith. Unless you could drop the antimatter bomb right next to the arcolith—at which point one could just use an ordinary nuclear bomb for the same explosive power—there was no danger to be had from antimatter weapons.

Unless...

Unless arcolite reacted differently to antimatter. Supposing there was a Fifth Force, might it have an inverse effect on antimatter? An antimatter bullet would still disintegrate. Yet, the antimatter released close enough to the walls of an arcolith might, in this hypothesis, be sucked in by the Fifth Force causing a detonation.

But there was no way of knowing if that was the case. And surely, even imagining his father had some reason to attack the arcoliths, he would not order such a costly project based on an unknown theory. Most likely, even if they threw all the antimatter they had at an arcolith, the explosion would barely crack the sides, not blow them up.

Satisfied, Anak closed his eyes and drifted back to sleep.

CHAPTER SIX

AS THE TILTROTOR TOOK HIM back to Lauriel's Arcolith, Anak idly browsed his copy of the *Summa Theologica*. It was hardbound, of course. He liked the feel of the crisp vinyl pages under his fingers, and he could have whatever he liked. He also liked to read in the original, even if he didn't know the language, so it was also bilingual: Latin on the left, Human on the right.

The children's education from Mr. Smith had included him telling them two creeds, both in dead languages. The first was of allegiance to the forgotten flag of a fallen nation, written in one of the precursor languages to Human. The second was in Latin, and Anak, remembering only small details, had looked it up again. Anak had studied enough Earth history to understand the meaning of the former. He was now learning the meaning of the latter.

Anak had always been vaguely interested in mortals' religions, ever since Mr. Smith had first introduced the concept. Philosophy was one of his favorite hobbies. So when he passed over the sheer audacity of arguing over nonexistent entities and ascribing personalities (no less than three of them) to Omnipotence, he found himself oddly drawn to theology.

He had, after discovering the sheer breadth and depth of Christian thought and its ensuing confusion and contradictions, decided to focus on the Roman Catholic teachings in particular. As both the largest and allegedly oldest denomination, it likely would have captured his interest. Mr. Smith's beliefs and his waiting room research further guided his choice.

His method was eclectic. Whatever struck his fancy, he learned. At the moment, he was interested in the history of the Church's dogma. He could explain the Nestorian heresy in detail, comparing it with the Orthodox position and putting it into historical context. He knew the twenty-two Ecumenical Councils and could recall what each discussed. He even understood how the addition of two words to a creed had split the Catholic Church in two, a division that still existed almost a millennium later.

More compelling to him were the debates. Anak discovered he had strong opinions over whether there was an Ixotak counterpart to the Angelic Virtue which guarded humanity, or whether the two were the same. He found himself mentally arguing over whether Christ (if He existed) would have had incarnated once for every species or once in each species.

But even more compelling than the debates were the practices. He was fascinated by how a simple action (the breaking of bread at the Last Supper) had become ritualized over two thousand years forming the Mass. He was surprised at how, in defiance of the Rationist heresy, naturally grown wheat and grapes were still used in their ceremonies no matter the expense. He was intrigued by the sheer dedication of priests who were required to say a special set of prayers several times every day, without fail, upon penalty of mortal sin.

Mortal sin. The idea was repulsive to Anak. The concept was simple: the intentional, knowing, commission of an evil act. The consequence, as taught by the Catholic Church, was also simple: damnation. Even the greatest saint, should he commit but one mortal sin, was in danger of hellfire if he did not repent.

Perhaps if Anak was not an immortal with responsibilities, his interest in the Catholic Church might have become more than academic were it not for that teaching. He might, if he was a mortal, even have considered its ideas seriously, were it not for that teaching. What could be worse, but to be on the ladder to Heaven, and then fall off it? Thomas Aquinas had even written (the *Summa Theologica*'s Question 94) that the Blessed would rejoice in the suffering of the Damned. How much more horrible would it be then, that your former companions would be happy to see you in Hell?

Not that Anak objected to Hell in principle. He supposed that those who lived and died without the love of Omnipotence (if there even was such a thing) in their hearts did not really have a right to complain that they would be forever cut off from it after death. It was the arbitrariness of those who had been otherwise good being condemned forever for even a single sin.

But it didn't matter, either way. He could not consider joining a mortal religion out of any personal desire, if he even had any, because he was immortal. His father would practically kill him. And, for the moment, he had more pressing things in mind.

But, he did have a strong, purely scientific curiosity towards that great ritual they called Mass. Though he could watch a hologram or video stream, he just didn't feel like it would be the same as being present. *Would Father approve?* he wondered. Well, nothing ventured, nothing gained. He wrote a short message asking for permission and sent it to the king.

Anastasia wasn't the only familiar face waiting for him in the dome outside the tiltrotor.

"Anak! How's it been?" Alexander asked. Unlike the other royals, he wore a green military jumpsuit on his short, thin body and a black cap over his cropped blond hair rather than furs and a crown. He stepped over and clapped Anak on the back. "I haven't seen you since last Council."

"I've been doing just fine," Anak said, following Alexander to the turbolift. "What've you been working on?"

"You'll see soon enough."

Anastasia was almost bouncing up and down in excitement. "Anak! Anak, listen! Father's finally going to give me a new assignment!"

"That's great, Annie," Anak said. "Do you know what it will be?"

"No, but he says it'll be important. And besides, I'm tired of being the secretary to the secretary."

The mortals knew them as Strategic Planning, but the Immortal Family called the annual meetings the Council of the Gods. Every immortal, no matter their age, would come to Lauriel's Arcolith to discuss the fate of humanity. Most of it was boring reports, such as the one that Anak would unfortunately have to make. But some of it was top secrets of the highest clearance. Though the mortals would consider it the highest privilege to be allowed to attend a Council, they now seemed banal to Anak, having grown up going to them. In any case, it was an excuse to visit with the Family.

The throne room was massive with a five-layer dais made of synthetic marble. A green and gold carpet, more of a tapestry on the ground, led from the throne to the great gilded double gates. In the corners of the room were four massive sculptures of double helices of DNA, the source and summit of the immortals' power.

Ninety thrones, some little more than cribs, for the Immortal Family filled the throne room. A massive holoprojector currently displayed the twenty-five arcoliths of Refuge with real-time data of every aircraft or crawler inside the Great Crater.

"The meeting shall come to order," Princess Cleopatra said. Her barbed tongue was more effective than any gavel. "We will begin with the Memory."

"Remember, my children, that Earth was once ours," King Oberon said, as he always did. "Mortal disagreements and mortal wars destroyed it, and only a remnant survived. We were saved by the Ixotak, but only just. One day when every argument has ceased, every problem solved, and death is no more, we shall return. And we will live to see that day."

"We work to bring that day," the others chanted in unison.

"We will now begin reading the minutes of the previous meeting," Princess Cleopatra said.

The only thing more tedious than these meetings, Anak thought, *is the recounting of the last meeting*. Then again, he didn't dare interrupt Princess Cleopatra.

Alexander's report was first on the agenda. He strode up to the holoprojector and gestured a few times, turning to a white wireframe depiction of the massive side of an arcolith. "This is what I've been working on for the past few months," Alexander said. "As you all know, my recent research has been in the AAD field, specifically in the EW and anti-PD area. The latest reports on the Union's new Ar2AiL platform show a increase of fifty percent on tracking speed..."

Anak had never been able to follow Alexander when he got into some military minutiae, especially when it was jumbled full of acronyms and incomprehensible abbreviations. This report was no exception. Whatever it was Alexander was on about, he became increasingly animated, talking faster with more wild gesturing. Princes Caesar and Napoleon seemed able to follow, if no one else, along with possibly the king and maybe Anastasia.

Then came a series of holographic images of red specks on the white wireframe. Green triangles flew towards the red; the two colors spewed dots and lines at each other. Some vanished as they were hit. Sometimes lines would fall from the heavens or emerge from the earth. This was mildly interesting, even if Alexander's commentary was still impenetrable to outsiders. At last Anak gleaned that it was a model of an aerial assault on an arcolith defended by ground-based lasers and Ixotak defense satellites. Then he realized it was several models in quick succession. At the end, they were going through models so fast Anak thought he might get a headache from the speed at which the lights flashed.

Finally came the last model, in which through a series of what Anak assumed to be tactical masterpieces all the red was destroyed. "...and that's why we need antimatter," Alexander finished.

"What?" Anak asked.

"Didn't you hear what I was just talking about?" Alexander asked.

"Um..."

"He is referring to the Rudra-class missile

prototype," King Oberon said with a bemused expression. "We can only get the explosive power we need if we use antimatter. More particularly, we need to know if we can fit a containment system on a missile."

"What? But we're making the antimatter for human war carriers! Why are we planning on attacking arcoliths?" Anak asked.

"It is a purely defensive measure," King Oberon said. "The other arcoliths see us and fear the future, the future that we shall own. If it ever comes to war, we must be prepared to invade another arcolith, and we must start by disabling its defenses."

"Exactly," Alexander said. "Now, the only problem is the missiles have to be pretty fast and pretty small with a lot of explosive power. That's why we need antimatter."

Anak opened his mouth and then shut it again.

"This is where you come in, Anak," King Oberon said. "We need an antimatter containment system that can fit on a missile. Are you able to make one?"

Anak thought. And, horribly, he saw it. It was a new puzzle like no other, one he would have to work on in secret. Room-temperature superconductors, on-board capacitors—the containment need only last for a second. It would be a challenge he would love, if only...

Well, it was purely defensive, right? "It may be possible, Father. I'd have to look into it."

"Consider this your new mission, then."

"Yes, Father."

"And speaking of new missions, I believe next on the agenda is Anastasia's new mission," King Oberon said.

"Yes, Father?" Anastasia asked, the eagerness in her voice undisguised.

Queen Titania answered instead. "We are the greatest work of humanity, yet our creators have grown restless. Mortalists grow bolder by the day, and the other arcoliths denounce our very existence. We must be sure that no matter what happens, the Eloi line is continued. Your job, Anastasia, is to provide this fail-safe."

"How, Mother?"

"You will go to a secret bunker distant from the arcoliths beneath the surface of Refuge. There you will be sealed inside with a number of loyal mortals. You will remain there in total isolation from outside contact. Should the worst happen, and we and our work are destroyed, you will wait, however long, for the situation to become safe for our kind again. Then you will reemerge to found a new Federation and create a new race of immortals."

"You have perfect memories of all the Immortal Family archive, and your blood contains the Eloi genes," King Oberon said. "There is none better to reconstruct our nation. I am sure that in this horrible and extremely improbable worst-case scenario that you will perform admirably."

"I'm to be a living time capsule, then?" Anastasia said with an unreadable expression on her face.

"A perfect metaphor," King Oberon said. "You will live, no matter what, to see the end of death. Even if we are cruelly murdered by the mortals, you guarantee that the Eloi will guide humanity into a new future."

"And... how long will I have to wait in this bunker?"

"If all goes well, only until the danger is passed. If it does not, as long as it takes."

"Given my life and training up to this point, I take it this was always planned for me," Anastasia said, her voice trembling slightly. It was so slight that Anak wondered if only someone as familiar with his sister as he was, noticed. "And I take it that there is no appeal from this decision?"

"Appeal? What are you talking about?" King Oberon asked. "We have gone too far along without fail-safes, and you were born for this very reason! Aren't you happy to have your purpose in life fulfilled?"

"No."

"No?" the King asked. "Well, I understand

this may be difficult to accept at first. It will be hard for Titania and I as well. We all appreciate your sacrifice."

"Sacrifice? *SACRIFICE!*" Anastasia screamed. "You plan and control every detail of my life, even from before I was conceived, sentence me to this without trial, and dare to thank me for 'my' sacrifice? What you are doing would be called child abuse if it wasn't for the future of humanity."

King Oberon blinked a few times. "Pardon?"

"No. I won't do it," Anastasia said.

"Anastasia, please—" King Oberon began.

"No."

"Be reasonable. Consider, as you said, the future of all humanity,"

"All I'm considering is what kind of sorry excuse for a father sends his daughter into something like this without remorse,"

"Come now, this is hurting us as well," Queen Titania said.

"It's your duty," Alexander said, "just as mine is to defend our kind."

"You cannot—you will not imperil the very fate of humankind with a childish sense of injury," King Oberon said.

"I can and I will," Anastasia ran out the double doors, slamming them behind her. Just under a hundred pairs of lime-green eyes watched her leave.

"Princess Anastasia Destruction Eloi

XIj17, you will return—" Queen Titania began to shout.

King Oberon waved her quiet, saying, "When she understands what we must do, she will comply."

"Father, surely—" Anak began.

"No. We will not have any more disagreement. Disagreement leads to strife, and strife to war, and war to death. We will not have death among the gods. Am I clear?"

"Yes, Father, but—"

"No buts!"

"...Yes, Father."

"My children, everything we must do is for the sake of humanity," King Oberon said. "Everything we do has been studied down the finest detail. If there is another way, it has already been considered and rejected. Whatever unpleasantness we must suffer to fulfill our destiny is only but a short moment of our eternal lives."

Is that really the case? came a seditious thought in Anak's mind. Has everything really been considered, or is this simply the easiest way out, no matter the consequences?

Anak found he did not disagree with the thought.

Anak searched all over the palace until

he found Anastasia crying in her massive, gilded room.

"Anastasia," Anak said, approaching the wooden-frame bed. "I'm... I'm, sorry."

"No, you're not. *You* aren't going to be frozen."

"What?"

Anastasia sat up. "Don't you know? They're going to put me under the stasis treatment. Like they did with Mr. Smith."

"But you're immortal. You don't need that to survive. You can wait centuries, even, and—"

"And go insane from loneliness? Or what if I run out of food? Or what if I trip and break a leg?"

"Um..."

"Some of the mortals there will be doctors and anesthesiologists, to put me under a Rachel Stasis. So that I'll be safe for however long it takes until it's time to rebuild the Federation."

"Well, the stasis is not technically being frozen—"

"Same difference!"

"But look; it's all highly unlikely that things would go this wrong."

"No, you listen! Father wouldn't do this unless there was a chance. And if there's a chance, it might all happen, and I'll wake up to find all of you dead! Or the stasis might go wrong, and then *I'll* be dead!"

"That's unlikely though—"

"No, it is *not!*" Anastasia picked up a pillow and threw it at Anak. She fell back into another pillow, sobbing.

Anak carefully put the pillow back on the bed. "Look, Annie, I'll... I'll find some way to convince Father."

"How?"

"There's bound to be a better way. There *has* to be a better way."

"You know how Father is."

"Yes, and he isn't insane. I convinced him to let me visit Mr. Smith, didn't I?"

Anastasia looked up with her tear-filled eyes. "Maybe. He wants me to leave for the bunker immediately."

"That's the first thing I'll convince him of, then."

———————

Anak caught his father just before he entered a meeting. "Father, one moment."

King Oberon stopped, the door-opening gesture halfway made. "What, my son?"

"It's about Annie," Anak said.

"Anastasia's mission is her mission. There will be no more disagreement on this subject."

"I'm asking for a week."

"A week for what?"

"A week to find a better way. It can't hurt, can it?"

King Oberon shook his head. "You realize that every day the arcoliths come closer to war? The final battle for humanity's fate may break out at any time."

"Yes, but the stasis procedure is risky, isn't it? If she dies, then there would be no failsafe. Isn't it worth just a little more time to ensure her survival?"

King Oberon looked directly into Anak's eyes, and Anak did not flinch. "I see. Your argument has merit. One week, no more."

"That's all I'm asking."

"Have it, then. Oh, and by the way, I granted your other request."

"What are you talking about?"

"Don't you remember? You wished to see a Mass. I approved it. The Roman Catholic Church has often been critical of our policies, if not our very beings. Nothing would throw them into more confusion than having one of us visit them at their highest ritual."

Anak had entirely forgotten. He didn't feel too much like engaging his curiosity, considering what was going on with Anastasia. Yet he could hardly refute the king's logic. "Of course, Father."

———◆———

He had no doubt as to which Mass to attend. It had to be Latin, as that was what Mr. Smith seemed to have preferred. To make the biggest stir among the mortals, he decided to visit the most ultra-conservative parish he could find. This turned out to be St. Michael's on Floor 542, a small, ancient but active ex-Old Terran church. He was even more pleased to discover that the celebrant, Father Orson, was the same priest who had visited Mr. Smith on the hospital floor.

Perhaps it was the incomprehensible language, said by the priest softly, or perhaps it was the too-strong incense. Perhaps it was the hardness of the steel pews and sitting on them for over an hour. Perhaps it was the awkward backward glances from the mortals at him and his guards. Perhaps it was that he felt out of place. Perhaps it was the sermon, which denounced the excesses of the LGF. Perhaps it was that his concentration was absorbed by thinking of ways to rescue Anastasia. Perhaps, he ironically noted, it was, in the words of G. K. Chesterton, "... very long and tiresome unless one loves God." Whatever the case, he had a terrible time. He was ready for it to be over shortly after the Gloria, and he could barely wait until it came time for the Prayer for the Ixotak.

When it was—finally—over, he remained to talk with the priest. He was amused and somewhat amazed that a mortal had enough courage to verbally attack his kind while he was in attendance. He was also concerned that the mortals were growing bolder.

"Ah, yes, Your Immortal Highness, is there anything I can do for you?" asked Father Orson when he exited the vestry.

"Why do you call me with such an exalted title, if you don't believe we're right?" Anak asked, the bluntness of his words surprising even himself.

The young priest shifted from foot to foot. "Erm, yes. That is, no, I don't believe you're right, sir. I am only giving honor to those whom honor is due, sir."

"Why?"

"It's scriptural, sir."

He must not have read that passage, Anak supposed. His father had assigned him and his batch-siblings parts of the Bible to read as homework. ("A cornerstone, if a false one, of Human literature and philosophy," quoth the king.) "I have a question," Anak said. "Why does the doctrine of mortal and venial sins exist?"

"That is also scriptural. First John chapter five, I believe."

"But why is it scriptural? Why was that book chosen as part of the canon?" Anak's next words came out with more emotion than he intended. "Why would a just Omnipotence damn his own children when they have only done one thing wrong?"

"Precisely because He *is* just, sir. Suppose I stole a credit and then gave two credits to charity. I have not come out ahead morally by one credit. I remain, until I am absolved, a thief undeserving of Heaven. No amount of rightness excuses a wrong."

"But 'love covers a multitude of sins.'"

"It is love that leads us to contrition, and contrition to forgiveness, sir. So, yes, it does."

"An interesting interpretation."

"The term you may be looking for is 'Final Preservation,' sir. That is, the grace that guarantees that one will not die without God in one's heart. There are several devotions approved by the Church that are said to grant this grace, such as scapulars, First Fridays, and—"

"While my time is unlimited, I have other responsibilities at the moment," Anak interrupted.

"Of course, sir. Though I must say that technically speaking, your time remains finite as even clinical immortals must one day—"

Anak struck him across the face with a fist. "Do not talk to me in that way, mortal!"

They stared at each other with anger. Anak looked down into the priest's eyes. Then slowly, deliberately, and without breaking eye contact, the priest turned his other cheek toward Anak.

Without another word, Anak turned and left.

———◆———

Anak returned to Facility 3-F. Saying nothing to anyone, he locked himself in his study. He searched for a way, any way, to save Anastasia.

His first idea was to have a copy of the Eloi genome and the Immortal Family Archive burned onto chips. These chips could be scattered in bunkers, satellites, and possibly on Refuge's moons, Hope and Memory. Future generations might destroy a few, but hopefully some would survive. Then when a new Federation arose, they could recreate the Eloi.

However, this was too passive. All their work would be staked on the chance that the future generation would seek humanity's destiny through immortality. Yet even some of the present mortals were against them. Who knew what they would do without immortals to guide them? If Anastasia were to be the backup, she could actively work to create a new Federation once she was reawakened.

Anak's second thought was to freeze several loyal mortals along with the chips, so that they could work in Anastasia's stead. The king vetoed this idea without explanation.

Anak's third thought was to put a sufficient number of mortals in the bunker with Anastasia—well, at that point it would be a bunker-complex. With a large enough population to avoid inbreeding, this colony would survive through the generations until it came time to retake the surface. In fact, there would be a small army for Anastasia to command.

King Oberon was delighted by this idea—except that it was long too late to expand the bunker secretly. Even then, it would be difficult to find the tens of thousands of mortals necessary. Anastasia wasn't impressed by it either. "I'll still live to see all of you dead, if the worst comes," she said.

"Then what do you want?" Anak asked.

"I don't... I don't want to be alone."

Days passed fruitlessly. There were other possibilities, which Anak rejected one by one. Perhaps they could bury another immortal with her—Father would not approve. Perhaps they could convince the Ixotak to take her—impossible. They could keep Anastasia at home until the danger came, then send her off in a tiltrotor—no use, it would be even more dangerous.

Perhaps she could be sent to another arcolith, but—

Wait.

That last idea had promise. Suppose Anastasia claimed to defect due to some imaginary mistreatment and "fled" to Aizokek's

Arcolith. (She could; she was a good actor.) Surely, if war broke out and all the immortals of the LGF were murdered, their enemies would not take the life of an innocent girl who had claimed sanctuary in a neutral arcolith. At worst, they might imprison her on some pretext or another, but she was immortal! One day she would be freed and then be able to rebuild the Federation.

The more Anak thought about it, the more he liked it. On the fifth day he gathered his thoughts together into a short paper and sent a copy to his father.

He got a reply an hour later. "My son, while your idea is excellent, it is too late. The schedule has been accelerated due to circumstances beyond our control, and Anastasia has already agreed to be sealed in the bunker."

Anak read and reread it five times and then threw his tablet with all his strength against the wall. Its screen broke into shards. "Clean that up," he told his guards, and then he sobbed.

CHAPTER SEVEN

THE LOSS OF ANASTASIA, ALTHOUGH he knew it was temporary, was more painful than Anak would have thought, even more painful than the deaths of his colleagues. Though he had his new mission, he found himself unable to concentrate.

Then there was the second explosion.

Anak had been in the control center, supervising the loading of the third shipment of antimatter. The antimatter was being sent from the facility to a top-secret depot by an automated crawler guarded by aerial drones. As per Anak's orders, no human was allowed close to the process.

A shielded lift carrying a Bowyer Trap full of antimatter was halfway to the surface when a technician swore loudly. A split-second later the floor buckled like it was being shaken by a giant. Inside the control center, chairs fell over with their occupants and terminals shattered. Anak himself fell over, but he was caught by his guards before he hit the floor.

"Is everyone all right?" Anak asked, getting back on his feet.

"No," someone groaned.

"Careful, there's glass everywhere," someone else said.

Anak pulled out his tablet. "Tablet, medical." He waited a few seconds. "Dr. Herbert? This is Director Eloi. There's been another explosion. Please prepare for wounded."

"Yes, sir," said the young doctor.

"Is anyone here severely injured?" Anak called out. "Call out if you are."

No one did.

"Everyone, head to Secondary Control, then," Anak said. "Let's find out what just happened."

"Sir, it was the lift," a technician said, slowly standing up. "I saw it lose power, and the Bowyer Trap lost containment. Sir, I'm sorry—"

It would have contained a gram of antimatter, producing a forty-three kiloton explosion. The shock wave had hit them *far* from the lift. What had it been like close by? "There's no use in self-recrimination," Anak said. "Let's go."

Twelve dead, and twenty-one wounded.

That was the final total. The shielding on the shaft had been a sick joke. Not a single life had been saved because of it. The radiation protection was irrelevant when the shock wave had traveled through it like an earthquake. Many of them, including Dr. Fredrick, had been crushed by heavy objects falling on them. Some, such as Dr. Wolf, had been knocked down staircases.

Anak forced himself to personally visit the overcrowded infirmary and nearby, the impromptu morgue. There were faces he recognized, though he didn't know the names, and faces he did not. All of them pained him, and he could not remove them from his memory.

He came back to the infirmary to find Dr. Ransom standing beside the bed of Dr. Wolf, and they were murmuring to each other.

"...Just about all my ribs are broken," Dr. Wolf was saying. "I won't be moving around for a while. I think this makes you full subdirector, now."

"Are you sure you won't be able to work from here?" Dr. Ransom asked.

"Not when I can't move my arms from traction, no. Did I mention my arms were broken? I think, I, in fact, did."

Anak tapped Dr. Ransom on the back. "If you have come here to gloat in any way—"

Their expressions told far more than their words as to their sincerity. "What are you talking about?" Dr. Ransom asked. "I was just expressing concern for my colleague."

"He has been an absolute gentleman," Dr. Wolf said.

"But you were calling for each other's resignations just a few weeks ago!"

"Mere disagreements do not reduce humane compassion." Dr. Ransom said.

"I wouldn't call them mere, but yes," Dr. Wolf said.

Anak shook his head. "I am amazed at you both. Please, continue."

"Excuse me, Director Eloi?" asked Dr. Herbert. He looked almost as bad as his patients. "Could I talk to you for a moment?"

"Very well." Anak followed him to an outside hallway.

Dr. Herbert sighed and said, "Sir, we are not equipped to deal with causalities on this scale. I know leaving is forbidden, but..."

"How bad is it?" Anak asked.

"Very bad, sir. I'm not a surgeon, and they need surgical care."

Anak closed his eyes. He hated making decisions like this. If he could, he would let his people return to the arcolith. But if he let them go, his father would be furious. "Suppose we brought in surgeons from outside."

"Maybe, sir. We'd—No, it won't work out. We would need to construct a whole hospital here. What are we going to do in the future when we need physical therapy? Or around the clock care?"

Aizokek's heads. He *hated* making decisions like this. His father would be absolutely enraged. But... he remembered the wretched sight of injured and horrible smells of the morgue. "Send them by tiltrotor back to Lauriel's Arcolith. I will deal with the regulations."

The relief on Dr. Herbert's face was incredible. "Of course, sir. Thank you, sir. I'll get them ready."

———————◇———————

Foresight had lead Anak to join the flight back to the arcolith. As the overcrowded aircraft took off, he waited in a private compartment for the call to come.

"I heard about the explosion at the plant," King Oberon said. He was sitting in the throne room on the other side of the screen.

Anak did not bother asking how. "There was one."

"Production must resume as soon as possible."

"Father, the facility is no longer safe. We need to redesign the facility entirely to prevent further accidents."

"Nonsense. It was perfectly safe before; it will be perfectly safe afterwards. Careless mistakes are just that: mistakes. Exceptions do not make a rule."

"Father, this is the second antimatter explosion we've had. We have over ten dead, in a facility of a hundred personnel."

"I see. Do you require replacement personnel, then?"

"Father, aren't you listening?"

"I am. And what am I supposed to do about mortal's mortality? Raise them from the dead? What is passed has passed." The king took one look at Anak's expression and added, "Don't give me that look. I ask again, what am I supposed to do?"

"Let us return to the arcolith with our injured."

"I see you are already on the way back."

"Of course I am, Father. It is medically necessary."

"You imperil the secrecy of our project."

"I imperil the lives of my people if I do not do this. Father, please—"

King Oberon scowled. "Fine. Do it. Come back with your wounded. But you must resume production as soon as possible."

"Surely—we must reconstruct things to be safer—"

"Impossible. Millions more and our very immortal lives will perish if we do not produce more antimatter."

"At least give me some more time to—"

"No. Resume production as soon as possible. Farewell."

———◆———

Two more died: one shortly after they arrived, one in surgery. The names were unfamiliar to Anak, but he blamed himself for both.

Waiting for more and worse bad news reminded him of that anxious time when Mr. Smith was put in stasis. The light green walls of the waiting room were even the same color as the one in which he waited that time. He now regretted that he did not see Mr. Smith's stasis unit when he had the chance. Then again, why not now?

He called Dr. Rachel. "Dr. Rachel? I'd like to see Mr. Smith's stasis unit. I am willing to put on scrubs."

Dr. Rachel blinked. "Erm, he is—he is currently in long-term storage. There'd be nothing to see."

"Ah. Nevermind. How is he doing?"

"Absolutely fine. Now, if you would excuse me, I am extremely busy."

"How so?"

"There has been a recent surge in new patients. We are putting three to five in stasis a day."

"Really? What caused this?"

"Ever since the news broke out of George Washington Smith asking for the stasis treatment, we've been flooded with applicants. We have to turn most away, unfortunately. Again, if you'll excuse me—"

"Of course. Thank you for your time. Farewell." Anak ended the call.

He had never thought about the other mortals asking for the stasis treatment. He supposed there were hundreds, thousands even, of those who needed it, and only a few who could receive it. Though it affected him in no way, he found that tragic.

As prince, he could do something about it.

———◆———

Shortly before he discovered the truth, he was on the palace floor in his room shifting through classified documents on his tablet.

The first step in solving an engineering problem was to define the problem. The problem was that the resources Dr. Rachel had were insufficient for the demand. But what were those resources?

Manpower would be one; he suspected they did not have enough doctors and nurses to put the patients into stasis and monitor and care for them. This could not be solved simply by throwing money at the problem for the personnel needed to be specially trained.

What else? Electrical power and supplies. No, those were unlikely to be limiting factors, but he made a note to check them anyway.

Space, however, would be the major limiter. For the sheer size of the arcoliths, space was still at a premium. Perhaps they could build extra-arcolithic facilities to hold patients? He decided to look up how much space it took for the stasis units to operate.

That information was buried deep in Dr. Rachel's somewhat disorganized research notes. There were different sized units to accommodate different body weights, as well as different experiments. Anak was more than slightly disturbed that they mostly seemed to be guessing the appropriate sizes. He hadn't imagined something so iffy when dealing with people's lives.

He also hadn't imagined that it was all a lie.

It was the numbers, in the end, that did it. Anak at last calculated that Dr. Rachel and her team had room for between two hundred and five hundred stasis units in the block of suites they occupied. *No wonder they have to turn away patients*, Anak thought.

Wait.

She had said that they had three to five new patients every day since Mr. Smith went under the stasis treatment. Mr. Smith went under it months ago. They would have filled their entire system by now. In fact, that wasn't counting all the patients they would have had *before* Mr. Smith. Something wasn't right.

He decided to double-check his figures, but he came up with the same numbers. Then he tried a different tack. He calculated what it took to power a number of what were essentially giant refrigerators and compared that to the power usage. He came up with even worse numbers. They couldn't have been powering up more than a hundred at a time. How was that possible? What was going on? *What had happened to Mr. Smith?*

With a feeling of horrible dread, he called Dr. Rachel immediately. "Dr. Rachel—"

She was already in scrubs on the other end of the screen. "My apologies, Your Immortal Highness, but I am about to commence another stasis treatment. If you would be as brief as possible..."

"I will. You are receiving three to five new patients every day?"

"Yes, sir. Sometimes more, sometimes less."

"And your stasis units use approximately half a kilowatt in power, correct?"

"I am not completely familiar with the electrical systems, sir, but that figure sounds correct."

"Your daily power bill is under fifteen hundred kilowatt-hours. That is enough to run less than a hundred and twenty-five stasis units. Your power bill should be several times its current amount, if you are using as many stasis units as you claim you are."

"I do not know, sir. Perhaps I am incorrect as to how much power a stasis unit draws?"

There was a slight hesitation in her voice, which Anak pounced on. "If you have somehow violated the laws of thermodynamics, yes. How many stasis units do you have?"

"I wouldn't know offhand, sir. A few hundred?"

"Of course a few hundred. You have been receiving at least a hundred new patients every month! You do not have room for a hundred new patients a month."

"I cannot see the problem with your math—"

"You are a college-educated doctor, and you are incapable of basic arithmetic?"

"Perhaps—"

"Perhaps you are lying to me. Let me ask you directly. What is going on? What is happening over there? *WHAT HAS HAPPENED TO MR. SMITH?*"

At this Dr. Rachel faltered. Her eyes had the look like one of the frightened rabbits on which she experimented. "I am, erm, I—"

"Answer me! I am a prince of the Immortal Family, and I will not hear any more lies!"

"I'm... I'm sorry, sir."

"Sorry for *what?*"

"The king ordered it, Your—Your Immortal Highness."

"Ordered *what?*"

"He asked me not to keep Mr. Smith. On the

king's orders, I gave him an overdose of the anesthesia medication. I assure you, sir, his death would have been absolutely painless."

"Painless?" Anak said. "A death is never painless for the ones who survive."

"Sir, the king—"

"No. I will not hear any excuses from you, you murderer!" Anak found he was standing, yelling, grasping his fists to the point of pain. "You murderer masquerading as a doctor, did your Hippocratic Oath mean nothing to you?" Before she could reply Anak chopped his hand in a diagonal slash ending the call.

Anak fell back into his chair and breathed heavily. Then the full force of the loss struck him. Mr. Smith was gone forever, and there was nothing he could do.

CHAPTER EIGHT

HE WANDERED THE PALACE LIKE he had wandered the facility once months ago, but this time without hope.

Mr. Smith was dead. The fact was like an iron ball he had swallowed, lurking in his gut, indigestible. Mr. Smith was dead and would never again tell Anak a story, or laugh at a joke, or wheeze and listen. Every memory Anak had of him was all that was left, and there would never be more. Mr. Smith was dead, and he no longer existed.

He wished he could believe that Mr. Smith was in a better place. He wished he could believe that Omnipotence had saved his soul. But how could he force himself to believe what he knew was not the case?

Perhaps—*perhaps*—it was. But why would reality conform to his wishes? Heaven, the hope of mortals, could not comfort him, an immortal.

And his father—his own *father* had done

this? Why? The betrayal hurt almost as much as the death. Why would he do such a thing?

No. There was no use wondering. This was a time for confrontation. He left for the throne room.

———————◆———————

The king was holding court in the throne room when Anak stomped in. Some luckless mortal was about to beg a favor from the king when Anak said, "Father, we must talk."

King Oberon seemed genuinely surprised. "What is all this about, my son? Can it not wait?"

"No," Anak said, and tried his best not to show the chaos of emotion inside of him.

King Oberon sighed, waving his scepter. "You are dismissed, all of you."

The courtiers turned to each other with confused glances and slowly backed out of the room. The petitioner swallowed his words and bowing, fled. The guards saluted and left. Only Anak and the king remained.

"Dr. Rachel has been killing her own patients," Anak said. "Anastasia is in danger."

"Your conclusion is incorrect," King Oberon said calmly. "But please, what evidence do you have?"

"She is lying about the resources she is using. There is no way, physically or mathematically, that she can have the number of patients she claims she has. Therefore, if she is lying about one thing, why not others?"

"You are partially correct," King Oberon said. "She indeed has fewer patients than she claims. The rest are—shall we call them 'test subjects'?"

"Test subjects?"

"We needed to perfect the treatment before we used it on ourselves. We never know what future eventualities might require us to seek some kind of stasis. With a wide enough variety of test subjects, nearly any conceivable scenario can be tested. Do you really think I would allow the use of the treatment on Anastasia without verifying its safety?"

"If that is so, why does she continue to kill patients?"

"We are testing more extreme scenarios."

"Father, that is—"

"That is what? Unfortunate? Of course it is. But these mortals are doubly doomed—first, because they are mortal, second, because of their old age or terminal illness. Their deaths, rather than being pointless, are all the more meaningful. And Mr. Smith is perfectly fine."

Anak heard himself say the words. "I know what you did to him, Father."

"Doubly unfortunate," King Oberon said with a sigh. "I was hoping you would have outgrown him by the time you found out."

"Outgrown him?"

"Oh, you know. Remember that book Anastasia used to carry around?" King Oberon scratched his beard. "What was it called?"

"*Piggins and the First Snow*? What ever happened to it?"

"I destroyed it. It was becoming an unacceptable attachment. Gods must not become chained to mortal things."

"Father, you—" Anak said.

The king's eyes flashed with anger. "Do not presume to argue with me. That Piggins book would have eventually worn out, I only accelerated the process. So would have Mr. Smith."

"He wouldn't *have* to! Father, listen!"

"Listen to what?"

"Our technology grows every year. One day we will be able not only to make ourselves immortal, but make others. What if nanobots could extend a mortal's lifespan indefinitely? What if we find some treatment that can regenerate the dying? What if—"

"But why would we do such things? We are already immortal."

"But the mortals—!"

"The Morlocks will pass on eventually. They all will, and we Eloi shall remain."

Anak thought for a second. "And would you 'accelerate' this process as well?"

"Wonderful," King Oberon said. "You are

the first to deduce the Grand Plan. I salute your intelligence."

Anak at first thought he had misheard. And then— "This is insane! You'd kill millions!"

"On the contrary, the Plan calls mostly for mass sterilizations after we rule Refuge. And even if we did kill millions, they were already dead in time."

"But... we're only one out of four neo-nations. We can't—"

"Ah, but your math is incorrect. The Automotocracy of Royale has joined us. Their vision is a future where no one has to work; our vision is one where no one has to die. They are entirely compatible."

"Surely we can't—by arcolith numbers we're still outnumbered."

"Not if we can disable enemy arcoliths. We call them arcobusters. A small antimatter charge, courtesy of yourself, will create a tiny crack in the surface of an arcolith into the inner nanobot layer. A certain kind of nanobot virus, developed by the Automotocracy, will then be inserted, 'poisoning' the arcolith and rendering it unusable."

Anak shook his head. "This is—I can't..."

"But you can! There is no mortal you are attached to, anymore. Come a hundred years from now and you will have forgotten all this. It is your destiny. You were chosen from before you were born for this!"

Anak's mouth moved, and no words came out.

"I suppose this will all be a shock to you," King Oberon said. "It is our only option, if we want to become truly immortal. I will send you the relevant section to your part in the Grand Plan over OTP. Your cooperation is necessary."

"I... Father, I..."

"Fear not. You may have a week to work out all your hesitations, like Anastasia did. Now, as you may have noticed, I was in the middle of something. Is there anything else?"

"N—No, Father."

"Then please, return to your facility and resume antimatter production. You can see how important it is to the future of humanity. The last of all human wars could break out at any time."

CHAPTER NINE

ALTHOUGH OUTWARDLY HE WAS BUSY giving orders for the repairs to the facility, inwardly he was dwelling on what his father wanted him to do. In his spare time he paced. His attempts to translate poetry or do anything else but think were fruitless. He read and reread his copy of the Grand Plan, ever seeking to see if it said anything other than what it did. Even his sleep was affected.

On the sixth day, Anak came to his conclusion.

His father was wrong.

He was wrong in what he said, wrong in what he did, and wrong in what he planned. There was no other word for it. Anastasia and Mr. Smith had been the first causalities in his mad plan, and unknown millions in wars and sterilizations would follow.

What was more, Anak was complicit in the manufacturing of antimatter. It was obvious now that the story of building human war carriers was only a fantasy. Anak could already feel the blood on his hands, staining them crimson in his mind. But what could he do?

He couldn't stop his father by himself. No words could convince him. And if Anak did not resume antimatter production, the king would surely find out. Anak did not have an army. Anak did not even have a single ally. He only had himself.

Anak supposed he could contact the other neo-nations, the Union and the League. But then that would only lead to the war starting earlier. With the arcobusters on the LGF's side, there could only be one conclusion: the king's victory.

What and who on Refuge *could* stop his father?

Except...

———————————

"Who are the Ixotak?" Anak once asked Mr. Smith.

"They're the saviors of humanity," Anastasia answered, before Mr. Smith could.

"I mean, aside from that," Anak said.

"No one knows for sure," Mr. Smith said. "All we cared about back then was that they'd take us out of what was left of Earth, and bless them, they did."

"But why did they do that?"

"Beats me," Mr. Smith shrugged. "Some

said that they they wanted to play god. Others said they wanted humans to do something for them eventually, but I can't imagine what we could do that they couldn't do themselves."

"But what do you think, Mr. Smith?"

"I think they wanted to do what was right."

"Can't we just ask them?" Alexander asked.

"Oh, y'all can message them all you want, as long as you're polite. They rarely reply."

"But they actually reply?" Anak asked.

"Sure they do. Not that they could reply to everything if they tried. People pray to them. They beg them. They want them to bring us back to Earth. They'd ask them to change our diapers, I don't know what."

"But why reply at all?" Anastasia asked. "They're so much far advanced than we are."

"Well, I figure if they looked kindly on us before, they'll look kindly on us again."

———— ◊ ————

Lauriel, hear me, a human.
My father has made antimatter
to ruin the other arcoliths.
Only you can stop him.
I beg you, help us.

That was the literal translation of what Anak thought of as his first poor attempt to communicate with the Ixotak. He went back and forth on whether to address the Ixotak all at once or to communicate with only one. If he did the former, the Ixotak might filter out the message as unimportant, regarding anything addressed to all of them as presumptuous or insane. If he did the latter, how did he know that the one Ixotak he addressed would be close enough or even able to respond?

At last he decided he would send it directly to Five-Commodore Lauriel, the assigned liaison of the Ixotak fleet to the human race. He would encrypt it with Lauriel's public key. Using the corresponding private key that only she possessed, Lauriel alone would be able to read it. The king would only know that a message had been through the transmitter, but not what it said or who sent it.

But what if Lauriel didn't arrive in time? She might be weeks, or for all Anak knew, months away. That was more than enough time for King Oberon to win the war and extinguish the mortals. Even the Ixotak could not bring back the dead.

Was there a way he could destroy the antimatter and the facility? He couldn't just blow it up with his people inside! Perhaps he could evacuate, and then detonate the antimatter? Yes, that was a good idea, but Anak's instinct was unsure.

Ah, yes. The spies. His father had at least one in the facility, and more likely more than one. If he simply evacuated, his father's spies could stay behind and prevent him from detonating the antimatter. Then it would all have been in vain. No, he needed to make sure the antimatter was gone and the facility destroyed.

Time! He needed more time! But *how?*

He needed another conspirator.

———————◇———————

"Yes, Director Eloi?" said Dr. Helen, entering his office and bowing.

Anak motioned to his guards. "Leave me."

"Sir—" began one.

"Leave me. I order it."

"Yes, sir."

Dr. Helen's face turned from curious to frightened. "Sir?"

Anak sighed. "The antimatter is being made for weapons."

Her pupils widened. "That's absurd! You yourself said—"

"I was wrong. Antimatter is the only way we can damage arcolite. The king plans to use it against the other neo-nations. He must have no more."

"But... but..."

"I am shocked as well. So, yes, I am now plotting against my father. I require your assistance."

Dr. Helen took a step backwards. "You—

you are asking me to commit treason! I could be executed for this."

"We might all be executed for war crimes if the king gets his way. This is our only choice if we wish to prevent another Final War."

"But..."

"Dr. Helen? Do you trust me?"

"...Yes, sir."

"Then join me. This is what we must do." He waved at the main terminal to a diagram of the facility. "I plan to contact Five-Commodore Lauriel. But until she arrives—"

"The Ixotak, sir?" Dr. Helen interrupted.

"Yes. We alone cannot stop my father. But until she arrives, we must ensure my father cannot use the antimatter, or produce more of it. If we place our remaining antimatter here, here, and here, as well as a few other locations, we can ensure that the resulting explosions will bring down the facility. The problem is, how do we ensure that my father's spies do not prevent this?"

"Your father—I mean, His Immortal Majesty—has spies here, sir?"

"Of course he does. I do not know their identities, but he has gotten information too fast." It belatedly occurred to Anak that Dr. Helen might have been a spy, but he had already taken the risk. "Can we mislead them somehow?"

Dr. Helen held her head. "Sir, this is all

too much for me. Is the king really planning another Final War?"

"My disbelief was similar. But we must concentrate. Think! What can we do?" Anak, in thought himself, waited.

"We could make it seem that we no longer have the antimatter, sir," Dr. Helen said.

"But how?"

"Send another set of Bowyer Traps to the depot, sir, only empty. Unless the depot has a very sensitive scale, the missing gram won't be noticed. Or we could fill them with normal hydrogen, and there'd be no way to tell."

"Perfect. That will work perfectly, Dr. Helen. But can we pull it off?"

Dr. Helen shrugged. "It would be dangerous, sir. We'd have to override the computers so it would place the empty traps into the crawler. I think our technicians would have to know. If any one of them is a spy, that's it for us."

"It will be a risk we must take. So, this is our current plan: We will send the empty traps to the depot. We will then sound the evacuation alarm. The spy or spies would have no reason to stay behind. When everyone is gone, we will then prepare the facility's destruction. Then we can detonate the antimatter and flee to another neo-nation. Veilvoid's Arcolith of the Union of Alpha would be the closest."

"Sir, that won't work."

"Why not?"

"By your very orders, sir, the control center computers are isolated from outside. Someone would need to stay behind to control the robots before making an escape."

Anak slapped his forehead. He knew there was something he was forgetting. "I must stay behind to prepare the detonation then."

"Sir, that's too dangerous. You're an immortal, and you could be killed!"

"If I can be killed, I am not technically an immortal. No, I cannot ask anyone else to risk their life. I must do it alone."

"As... as you wish, sir. I cannot say I agree. And, sir, I would suggest you read the technical manuals. You will need to keep at least one fusion reactor running while you set up the explosion, or we will lose containment in the Bowyer Traps."

"Of course. Now, please, prepare the decoys. We will need them immediately."

———◆———

Anak had never lied to his father before, and he didn't know if he could believably do so. So he just wrote a message: "Dear Father, since our last shipment was interrupted, we still have over a hundred grams of antimatter left in the facility. Please send an automated crawler to receive the next shipment."

"Of course, my son," was the reply less

than an hour later. "The crawler is already on its way to you."

———————◆———————

His plan was set. After this, there was no going back.

That is, he reminded himself, if he decided to go through with it at all.

He rapped his fingers on his desk. He didn't know how his father would respond, but he would find out soon enough. And then what?

If he failed, he would be imprisoned for a long time, centuries perhaps, until he came to see the same view as his father. More likely, if he failed, the king would put him under stasis like Anastasia so that Anak could do nothing until the immortals won. There was a chance the stasis treatment might fail, or he might get killed by accident. Or he might fail to escape the destruction of the facility. And then he would be dead.

What was non-existence like? Anak supposed he would never know, being that he would not exist when it happened. He supposed that he had not existed before his birth, and that was not so horrible. Then again, he was nothing before his birth, and now he had something—everything—to lose.

From the position of rational self-interest, his own death would be valued as an infinite loss. Every good thing that he might experience was contingent upon his continued, immortal existence. Logically, his survival would be more important than the survival of *Homo sapiens*, no matter how tragic the species' extinction. Perhaps he should forget his plans, contact Father, and continue with the Grand Plan.

Perhaps as Mr. Smith would have said, that was all a load of baloney.

He opened his message to Lauriel and pressed send.

CHAPTER TEN

THE NEXT WEEK ANAK SPENT in second-thoughts and recriminations. He was destroying his life work. He was betraying his father. He might not even succeed. He might *die*. These thoughts and more lingered in his mind day and night. He thought about it when they loaded the fake traps onto the crawler. He thought about it until the crawler was one day away from the depot, and he had to continue willingly with the plan.

Anak was in his office, waiting until he could wait no longer. "Guards?" he said. "I want you to look at something."

"Yes, Your Immortal Highness?" one asked.

Anak handed his tablet over to them. "Read this. Both of you."

After a few moments, one looked up. "Sir, this is classified information, we shouldn't..."

"Look, you idiot," the other said. "Read it."

"It's the genuine document," Anak said. "The king plans the end of the mortal race."

"But—but sir," the first guard said. "I'm in the highest class. I'm guaranteed three children! My genes will be mixed with the Immortal Family's DNA bank—"

"The latter has always been a lie. Mortal DNA is never used to create us. And the former will be a lie soon enough. I am an immortal telling you this. Do you not believe me?"

"No. This—this is some kind of loyalty test, isn't it?"

"It is not."

The other guard had a panicked look. "We're all going to die?"

"Not if I can help it. Flee this facility while you can. Both of you. That's an order."

"But what about you, sir?" asked the first guard.

"Do not worry about me. I have a plan. Speaking of which... Main Terminal? Sound the evacuation alarm."

The shrill, deafening sound pierced the guard's next words.

Guard two grabbed guard one by the arm. "Go!"

"But—"

"GO!" shouted Anak.

The guard bowed, shaking, and left. Anak hoped the best for the two of them. He never had learned their names.

Anak motioned the door to close and lock, and then turned to his tablet. With a few taps he deleted his entire copy of his research. Then, he uploaded a prepared file of nonsense to the Immortal Family archive as an 'update' to his notes.

He took a few deep breaths. There, he had done it. All copies of his research data were gone. King Oberon could not build another factory with Anak's design. He would surely find out what Anak had done.

His second prepared file contained a copy of Dr. Rachel's research notes, with the inconsistencies highlighted. He sent that to the Aizokek's Arcolith News Network.

He dithered on whether or not to send his third prepared file. It contained a copy of the Grand Plan, and it was addressed to the security agencies of the Union and the League. At last he supposed that it didn't really matter at this point. The fate of the other neo-nations rested on whether he could delay his father's attack, and if the Ixotak arrived in time. But even if both should fail, at least they would not be surprised by the attack that would defeat them. He sent it.

He brought up the diagram of the facility. The lights indicating the personnel still inside converged on the lifts and left. As soon as the last was out of sight, Anak grabbed his tablet, got up, and ran to the secondary control center. It was time to move the antimatter into place to destroy the facility.

It was eerie, running down the corridors with no one in sight. Just as he reached the final door, his tablet rang. He put it on speaker. "Hello, Father."

"I trust you have some explanation for your actions," King Oberon said. "I hope you are not throwing a tantrum over the death of a mere mortal."

Anak swiped his card, stepped into the abandoned control center, and walked to the robot control station. He was unfamiliar with the controls, but the movement routines were obvious enough. He started typing. "I cannot bring back Mr. Smith, but at least I can stop the end of the human race."

"And how do you plan on accomplishing this?"

"You'll find out soon enough."

"Come now, are we not even more human than the Morlocks? Do we not represent their greatest desire: immortality?"

"Mortal or not, it is not right to kill the innocent."

"Then all the more reason for us to survive. Are we not acting only in self-defense?"

"You call a preemptive strike self defense? You call *genocide* self-defense?"

"All the mortals are doomed anyway. It is only ourselves who might escape that fate. Think! Do we not have within our grasp the

Matthew P. Schmidt

ultimate goal of life: eternity? Should we not take what is rightfully ours?"

"Not this way. It isn't right." Anak watched through the screen a robot loading a Bowyer Trap into itself then crawling off to its designated location. Satisfied, he walked over to the reactor control station and watched it carefully. He had had to take a crash course on reactor management, and he was still fuzzy on the finer details. He could only hope that nothing would happen to take all five reactors offline, causing the Bowyer Traps to lose containment.

"Who cares about the morality of it, except ourselves? The mortals? They will die anyway. The Universe? Omnipotence? It does not care."

"I care."

"Why should you? You are not a moralist, now, are you? Have you come to the delusion that there is objective morality in the universe?"

Anak thought for a moment. "It appears that I have. Mr. Smith believed it."

"Mr. Smith is dead! He is no more! My son, you have been driven insane by him."

"There is someone insane in this conversation, and it is not I."

"Nonsense upon nonsense. I am acting perfectly rationally."

"How so?" Anak asked.

"How *so*? I will live forever, and all my

126

actions are for this very goal. That is the very definition of rationally: acting according to reason. And is it not reasonable for immortals to be immortal?"

"We are not truly immortal. Even if you succeed, what do you imagine will happen in the next five thousand years?"

"I will be alive and quite happy about it," King Oberon said.

"And you will not have died from any accidents, or assassination attempts, or illnesses, or mistakes?"

"The chance of any of those things—"

"But there is a chance. No matter how unlikely, given enough time, everything that might happen will happen. And some day, we will die."

King Oberon laughed. "Is that what you are concerned about? Let us pretend we will live only a million years, pretend, I add. Does it even matter?"

"It matters on the three hundred sixty-five millionth day."

"But would our lives not be worth that of a million mortals?"

"No."

"How so?"

"The shortness of a life has nothing to do with its value."

"Nonsense. The more life, the more value it has."

"Perhaps so. But no one deserves to live by killing others."

"It will only be a moment. A few hundred million deaths, then no more death every again."

"It is still wrong," Anak insisted.

"This conversation is going nowhere," King Oberon said. "What do you think you will accomplish with this insanity? We have enough antimatter to win the war. You sent the last necessary shipment!"

"That shipment contained nothing. And even with the antimatter you already have, without my design abilities, I don't think you can make an antimatter missile, either."

"I have a thousand scientists at my beck and call. We can make the missiles with or without your help."

"Yet you asked me to make one. Perhaps you fear your thousand mortal scientists might turn on you?"

There was a short silence on the other end of the line. "Irrelevant. The missile is only for convenience. We can simply deliver the antimatter to the target some other way. The enemy arcoliths will still fall, and we will still win the war."

"Perhaps you will have destroyed the arcoliths, but you will not win the war."

"Have you become the military expert,

now? Alexander will be so happy to learn that his batch-brother has the same interests."

"Do you think all the might of the LGF and the Automotocracy can fight off a single Ixotak war carrier?"

"Now your delusions include the Ixotak? Pray tell them to me."

"I messaged Five-Commodore Lauriel a week ago. Surely she is on her way right now to stop you."

"But why would she do that?"

"Excuse me?"

"Are not the Ixotak immortal? Have we not seen the same twenty-five names again and again? They have no doubt discovered how to make themselves immortal and have already eliminated their own mortals."

Anak had not thought of this. But no, he had gone too far now. "Even if she will not come, it is still right to try. I will not stand for this. I will not be complicit with genocide."

"Is that your final answer? Will you not repent, my son?"

"You, Father, are the one who must repent."

"Do you realize that I can kill you, right now?"

CHAPTER ELEVEN

A NAK TRIED NOT TO LET any emotion show in his voice. "How?" he asked.

"I have moved a combat mirror satellite in alignment. With the press of a button, I can fire the gigawatts of main defense laser batteries of Lauriel's Arcolith into space, have them bounce off the mirror, and drill beneath the surface to incinerate you. I already know your location from your tablet's broadcast. In fact, allow me to demonstrate. Please do not move."

All Anak heard was an indistinct rumble, and then an explosion behind him. He spun to see that the steel door—the only door—was bent and glowing molten red.

"As you might have noticed, the corridor outside your control room is now full of melted silicate, ionized gas and metal fragments. There is no escape."

"You'd really kill me?" Anak's voice was hollow. "*Me?* Your own son?"

"My son, I have already spared you once."

"When? I do not remember—"

"—of course you do not, you ungrateful brat. Have you never wondered why you are so large?"

"I assumed it was a mild case of immortality induced gigantism, similar to what killed the first six batches of the Immortal Family. Without cellular death, the body can only grow."

"Indeed you are correct. And you never wondered why your embryo was not culled? It was I who saved you, I who said we had lost too many of batch XI already, I who ordered you spared."

"Then I must thank you, Father, but—"

"You force me to destroy you! There must never be disagreement between us, lest there be conflict, war, death. There must only be agreement."

"That's untrue, Father."

"What?"

"I have seen mortals set aside their differences, even those who have the greatest hatred towards one another. Surely we can do the same?"

"Nonsense. You have become a mortal in thought, word, and deed. But come, there is still time. Return to me, and I will save you."

"I will not."

"Then you must die."

"We all must die."

"Why are you even acting this way? Are you not afraid of death?"

"Father, ever since I learned that I could die, I have been afraid of death."

"Then why—"

"I am not stronger than my fear. But there are stronger things even than that."

"Like what?"

"Love."

"Love?"

The next words spilled out of his mouth. "'Greater love hath no man than this: to lay down his life for his friends.'"

"My son, the mortals are not our friends."

"My people are my friends, and you did not want to let me save them. Anastasia was my friend and sister, and you froze her. Mr. Smith was my friend and mentor, and you killed him."

"All true," the king admitted, "but irrelevant. Life is the highest value. You are throwing away that which is of most value."

"Perhaps. But I think love is more important than life. Life passes away, but love, never."

"Love will perish at the end of the universe."

Anak paused for a moment. And then, he said, "I know not why the universe is. But if I could explain it, I would love it—that explanation, that Truth. Truth is inherently lovely. But what loves it? Surely the Truth loves Itself. And if Truth can love, surely it has loved me first."

There was silence on the other end. "Are you absolutely out of your mind?"

"My great learning, I suppose, has driven me insane."

"Come back, Anak! Do not do this!"

"If I must die, even if I cannot stop you, even if the Ixotak will not stop you, even if all is lost, I will at least die for a reason." Anak reached for a prayer and could only come up with the first one he had learned: the Latin Creed. *"Credo in Deum Patrem omnipotentem; Creatorem coeli et terrae."* I believe in God, the Father Almighty, Maker of Heaven and Earth.

"Stop."

"Et in Iesum Christum, Filium eius unicum, Dominum nostrum, qui conceptus est de Spiritu Sancto, natus ex Maria Virgine." And in Jesus Christ, His only Son, Our Lord, who was conceived by the Holy Spirit, and born of the Virgin Mary.

"Stop, my son. All will be forgiven, only stop."

"Passus sub Pontio Pilato." He suffered under Pontius Pilate.

"Please, Anak, do not make me do this."

There was a pause, as wide as the gap between Heaven and Hell.

Anak thought. He thought of Mr. Smith and all he had done for him. Every joke, every shared laugh, every letter, every lesson. He thought of the way he used to say things in that strange accent of his, or the time that he tried, poorly, to sing the anthem of his long-dead nation.

He thought of his time as an immortal. He thought of the many privileges and honors that had been his since birth. He thought of his gene-foretold destiny, that he would be a great scientist, and look at him now! He thought of how he would be the greatest of his generation, perhaps, and his fame would be remembered as long as the immortals lived.

He thought of Anastasia, her life, her destiny that was chosen against her will. He thought of the time they had spent together, even their arguments, even their fights. He thought of her laugh, her smile, all now frozen in some stasis chamber in some bunker far away.

He thought of his workers, his colleagues, his team. He thought of how he had assembled them himself, each specially chosen for their skills. He thought of what would become of them now.

He thought of the Church, her pious legends, her ancient traditions, her theology. He thought of the LGF, its work, its power, its achievements, and maybe soon, its victory. He thought of all the things he had left undone, knowing he would live forever. He thought of the things he ought to do, even though his death would come from them. He thought of Alexander and his whole-hearted embrace of his duty. He thought of Dr. Helen and her service even into committing treason with him. He thought of his favorite food, mashed potatoes, and how he might never eat them again.

He thought of how he had never resolved his misgivings about the Church's teachings, and here he was about to die a martyr if he so chose.

He thought, at last, of St. Dismas, the Good Thief crucified, and his dying words to Christ. "Jesus, remember me when you come into your kingdom."

All these thoughts passed in one long moment, in a silence of which he would never understand the depth and width. "Anak?" King Oberon said. "Are you still there?"

Anak pulled out his tablet and set it on an empty spot on the control panel. He looked into his father's eyes, and said, "You don't need to do this."

"Thank you, Anak, you—"

"Unless you chose to do so. *Crucifixus, Mortuus, et sepultus, descendit ad inferos, tertia die resurrexit a mortuis, ascendit ad caelos, sedet ad dexteram Patris omnipotentis.*" He was crucified, died, and was buried. He descended into Hell. On the third day he rose again. He ascended into Heaven, and is seated at the right hand of the Father Almighty.

"Anak, no! Do not do this!"

Anak heard the rumbling again, and closed his eyes. *"inde venturus est iudicare—."* He will come again to judge the—.

While the laser missed Anak by several meters, the expanding cloud of plasma killed him instantly. The plasma flashed across the control center and turned the terminals, chairs, and everything else into super-heated goo. A second later, the structure damaged beyond repair, the ceiling collapsed.

For all its accidents, the facility had been designed with absolute safety in mind. However, it had also been designed in parts, each classified design holding only a section of the whole. The fusion reactor designers, not knowing how vital continued power would be, had designed them to shut down automatically in case control was lost.

The damage from the earlier accident to the control center computers in Primary Control had not yet been repaired. As their twins in Secondary Control were melted and then crushed, the encrypted signal to the fusion reactors was lost. The reactors followed their programming and, as intended, deactivated.

The robots had moved only a fraction of the antimatter into place. The rest, located in the vault, lost containment. The three megaton explosion shook the facility and detonated the remaining antimatter with its shock wave. With structural support lost, the facility fell in on itself and, along with the antimatter, ceased to exist.

EPILOGUE

Defectors Claim LGF was Producing Antimatter Weapons! read the headline.

Famed physicist Dr. Miriam Windsor Helen and almost a hundred other scientists and skilled technicians were received today by the Union of Alpha. Citing the recent laser strikes, explosion, and minor earthquake outside of the Great Crater as evidence, they say they were involved in a secret antimatter production project. The whereabouts of the alleged director of the project, LGF prince Anak Og Eloi XIa11, are currently unknown. A spokesperson for the Immortal Family was unavailable for comment...

A second article read "Famed Stasis Doctor Embroiled in Scandal, Accused of Killing Own Patients."

Recently leaked documents, allegedly from the Immortal Family's archive, implicate Dr. Candace Lorenz Rachel, the anesthesiologist responsible for the first successful human cryogenics, in killing her own patients. So far, the Lauriel's Arcolith Security Department has said they can neither confirm nor deny they are investigating these allegations. Dr. Rachel herself has denied all charges. The Society of Terran Remembrance has expressed concern as to the safety of George Washington Smith, the oldest remaining Survivor, who was placed under a stasis treatment in May...

———◊———

In a distant system, the war carrier *The Many Victories of Omnipotence* was mining an asteroid for useful materials. With those she made weapons: combat mirrors, missile-drones, new exterior railguns and lasers to replace those lost in the last battle against the Foe. It was a perhaps undignified task for such a massive and majestic vessel, but she had been designed to survive alone, even if she was the last vessel of its kind.

Aboard the starship, in the very center of

the core, Five-Commodore Lauriel was shifting through her mail. Much of it, to human eyes, was sweet thanksgiving and adoration, or less commonly curses and imprecation for failing to do this or that. Some were the messages of the ambivalent. Some were the messages of the insane. What Lauriel thought of this, humans could only speculate.

Rarer than praise or blame was every human trick employed to glean information from her. Some were demands: the secrets of arcolite, the methods of antimatter production, the physics of FTL travel, the design of general purpose nanobots, the blueprints of war carriers. Many tried hiding their wishes in pleas for assistance, begging her to consider their common bond as intelligent life. Many more asked for what the Ixotak said was impossible: causality breaking, zero-point energy, true immortality, godhood.

Some tried providing the latest hypotheses and asked if perhaps one of these might be correct? Might you clarify a constant? Or they would ask a hundred and twenty-five questions, hoping that a single answer, or lack of one, would give them the wanted facts.

Others were curious about the Foe, or how the war against them faired, and asked if they could know how and when they would return to Earth. They asked politely, sometimes not, if they could have the smallest bit of tactical data, or a war drone to study, or even a general explanation of how war was made in space. They suggested they could provide advice, even assistance. A few one would go as far as to give it anyway, offering ideas and blueprints for weapons, with the hope that one might prove even slightly useful.

A small amount was humans providing information to her that might be considered, by humans at least, to be useful or interesting. Poems, puzzles, games, diaries, commentary on the Cultural Dump, or humans sometimes explaining their own idiosyncrasies. These rarely received replies, which was a better response than most communication with the Ixotak.

Smaller still was news, both true and rumor. All major news services, and most minor ones provided copies of their data to her, and would even attempt to translate it into Ixotak. On the most odd occasions she would send a request for more information, a happening that usually became more noteworthy than the story itself.

At last she came to the message.

> "Lauriel, hear me, a human.
> My father has made antimatter
> to ruin the other arcoliths.
> Only you can stop him.
> I beg you, help us."

Ixotak thoughts are not human thoughts, and it would be useless to speculate how she thought on the matter. But she did think, and after some time motioned with a false-head to open the log. She said, in the dancing language of the Ixotak, *"These creatures whom we saved / have returned to their folly, / common to all thinking beings. / I return to stop them. / Pray I arrive in time."*

Another false-head touched the command shackle a few times, and *The Many Victories of Omnipotence* prepared to fire her massive engines on a course for Refuge.

"—Credo in Spiritum Sanctum, sanctam Ecclesiam catholicam, sanctorum communionem, remissionem peccatorum, carnis resurrectionem, vitam aeternam. Amen. " I believe in the Holy Spirit, the Holy Catholic Church, the Communion of Saints, the forgiveness of sins, the resurrection of the body, and life everlasting. Amen.

Anak finished, opened his eyes, and saw Omnipotence. He would never have imagined that He would have such beautiful blue eyes.

"Welcome home," He said.

"I hoped, but I wasn't expecting this," Anak admitted. He felt he should kneel, and he did so. "I thought—I don't know. Maybe it was all false, but it was worth a shot. I'm sorry."

"You were forgiven long ago."

Anak looked behind Him, and saw thousands, millions, uncountable numbers, of humans in white robes outside the gates, wearing crowns of rubies and gold. Anak saw Ixotak, too, with white-and-ruby shackles on their false-heads, and they stood by other, stranger, creatures. Anak was somehow not surprised to see other races there, but amazed at their variety.

Above and all around were angels of every kind and shape. There were winged beasts covered with eyes, flying by massive wheels bejeweled with gems of more colors than Anak thought possible. There were angels as tiny as fairies, and angels so huge Anak mistook them for clouds at first. He could hear their wings flapping, and the voice of their choirs, all singing, all in harmony: *Holy, Holy, Holy.*

"Anak!" a young man said and hugged him.

"Who are you... Mr. Smith?" Anak asked and looked to Mr. Smith's side. A young woman stood there. "You must be Carol." Anak looked to his own side and saw a figure clothed in light. "I take it you are my guardian angel?"

"Yes," the being said. "I am now the angel with whom you will rule—you need a guardian no longer."

Anak turned to his other side, and for a moment thought he saw his father. But no, it had wings and though it had lime-green eyes, its hair was white. "And you are...?"

"I am the Angelic Power that guards your subspecies. My name is—" and the Power said a word so beautiful Anak was surprised he understood it completely. "—You are the first of your kind to arrive here. Congratulations."

There was also another man there, whom Anak recognized after a moment. "Father—Orson? Why are you here?"

"What, did you expect me in Hell?" asked the priest, who laughed. "Your father arranged for my death after that incident where you hit me. I take it he was afraid that a mortal might be an immortal's moral superior."

"Oh. I am sorry about that," Anak said.

"There is no need, here."

Anak thought. "But—Wait, what about my father? What about Refuge? What will happen to humanity?"

Omnipotence shook His bearded head. "Fear no longer. Trust in me. Whatever you pray of me here, I will do."

"Then—then save them. Save us, the immortals."

"All will be well." He stretched out a hand holding a white stone, and with the other he crowned Anak. "This is your new name."

Of that name, no one knows except Him and Anak himself, and it would be unwise to speculate. But perhaps it said something like this: "Prince Anak Og Eloi XIa11, first martyr of the immortals."

ACKNOWLEDGEMENTS

Many thanks to my mother for providing invaluable editorial assistance, my brother Nathan for his ruthless critiquing, Bonnie Oliver for several great ideas, and my father for moral support. Loves!